Just One Kiss

A Kingston Family
Dirty Dare Story

NEW YORK TIMES BESTSELLING AUTHOR

Carly Phillips

JUST ONE KISS

**It was supposed to be one fun night of hot sex.
It turned into a second. Then a third.
Now Mother Nature is having the last word—with
a secret baby surprise!**

Jade Dare has done everything in her power to overcome her mother's unstable influence. Changed her name. Became a success. Vowed never to risk passing on the potential for inherited pain. What has it gotten her? One fiancé who wanted her for money. A second who cheated on her with his brother's wife.

Now she's sworn off men. Or at least off serious relationships. But when the chance to indulge in a one night stand with a man she's secretly fantasized about arrives, she jumps in. Only to land heart-first into a case of the feels she can't bring herself to trust.

Knox Sinclair always suspected he liked his brother's fiancé a little too much, that's why he kept his hands to himself. But with ties broken and Jade all too willing, a no-strings-attached night sounds like a damned good idea.

Except one night isn't nearly enough. But while Knox is busy convincing Jade they have a chance at forever, the past is planning one last parting shot.

To my readers: To those who are sensitive to the topic, this book contains discussions of suicide that occurred in the past. For anyone in pain or in need, here are resources to help. Please don't suffer alone.

National Suicide Prevention Lifeline
Hours: Available 24 hours. Languages: English, Spanish.
800-273-8255

For more information:
The Keith Milano Memorial Fund
https://keithmilano.org

Chapter One

THE SUN SHONE overhead as Knox Sinclair pulled into the parking lot designated for people attending the Bridal and Wedding Expo in New Jersey. After finding a spot, he cut the engine and turned to his newly engaged stepsister, Holly, who was sitting in the passenger seat, her body vibrating with excitement. She couldn't wait to get in there... unlike Knox, who avoided anything wedding related ever since his marriage had imploded more than a year ago.

Was he over his ex? Yes. Did he carry a grudge against his cheating former wife and disloyal stepbrother? Also, yes. Any rational man would.

"Ready?" he asked Holly.

Her brown eyes lit up, making Knox's feelings about the Bridal and Wedding Expo irrelevant. To Holly, this was important. And he would be there for her.

"Beyond ready! I can't wait to check out all the booths," she said. "How awesome is this going to be?"

He held back a sarcastic reply because he loved his younger sister. "Too bad Miles isn't here to walk you around," he said of her future groom, a mergers and acquisitions attorney who was currently on a business trip.

Reaching over, Holly patted Knox's cheek. "Good thing you love me and are willing to take his place. Come on. It's going to be fun!" Holly unhooked her seat belt and opened her car door, turning to face him before letting herself out. "Besides, you know you'd do anything for me. I'm the baby of the family."

He rolled his eyes. "Someday that reasoning is going to wear thin," he said, chuckling. But she was right.

He'd adored Holly the day he'd first met her. Knox and his father had opened their home to a four-year-old Holly, her thirteen-year-old brother, Theo, and their mother, Knox's father's new wife, Addison. Holly had been adorable and exuberant, and she'd latched onto Knox immediately.

She'd been in need of an older brother, and even at fourteen years old, Knox had patience where Theo had had none. The selfish bastard still rarely bothered with his sister. Then again, it seemed as if the only person he cared about was himself.

"No, it won't." She grinned and hooked her arm in his.

He resisted the urge to rub the top of her head, the way he used to do when they were kids, knowing she'd be annoyed if he messed up her hair.

Their parents had separated when Holly was eighteen and in college. Knox's dad had died shortly after the divorce was finalized, leaving everything to Knox, including the football team he owned. The New York Warriors were in Knox's blood. And Holly was his family. Knox had taken it on himself to support his sister, whose mother had disappeared to Palm Springs with yet another wealthy man and her father had passed away. Today was her day. Knox was just happily paying for whatever choices she made.

"Let's go." She started toward the building, and he matched her shorter strides. When they reached the doors, he opened one for Holly and allowed her to precede him. Then, together, they walked inside, and the cool air-conditioned lobby shocked him into paying attention.

"We need to sign in and get our badges." Holly led him over to the end of a long registration line and he settled in to wait.

She rose onto her tiptoes and looked around, trying to see above the crowd in front of them.

"Looking for something?" he asked.

She sighed and turned back to face him, a pout on her lips. "I was looking for a display of maps or brochures, but I guess we'll get everything we need when we register. I want to check the layout of the exhibit. I already know which vendors I want to see but I have to find their locations. And I especially want to talk to Jade."

"Jade?" His brain came to a halt at the name, and his cock jerked in excitement.

"Come on, Knox, you know. Theo's ex," Holly said.

Yeah, he knew. *Jade Dare.* The woman who'd experienced the same betrayal he had. And the woman he'd been seriously, dangerously attracted to—even though he'd been committed to making the most of a shitty marriage with a wife he could never make happy.

He recalled the night Theo had walked into the restaurant where Knox and Holly had been having dinner, with a familiar *I'm up to something* smirk on his face and a beautiful young blonde on his arm. Knox hadn't recognized her until their introduction. Prior to that moment, the last time he'd seen Jade, she'd been a teenager. Knox had attended business school with her brother and his good friend, Asher Dare, and they'd all been at Asher and Knox's business school graduation.

The female with her arm hooked through Theo's had grown into a gorgeous woman. She possessed a statuesque body, long, wavy hair he wanted to wrap around his hands, unique navy eyes that ran in her family, and plush glossed lips he'd been dying to kiss. Finding out she was Asher's younger sister had been a shock.

Seeing her with Theo had been a gut punch that had made him unexpectedly determined to look out for her. Few women escaped Theo unscathed. Since Knox had been married at the time, he'd kept his opinions—and his desire—to himself. However, he had warned Asher to keep an eye on the new man in his sister's life. Still, even Knox had never dreamed how low his stepbrother would go.

"Knox?" Holly waved a hand in front of his face. "Where did you go?"

"Sorry. Yes, I remember Jade."

"Of course you do." Holly tucked a strand of her shoulder-length brown hair behind her ear. "You had a thing for her," his sister said, as if his feelings had been obvious.

"Don't be ridiculous. I was married when we met," he said, stepping forward to follow the people in front of him.

Holly did the same, then turned to him again and tilted her head. "*Right*. You were married to that horrible woman. But you weren't dead. Of course you noticed how beautiful Jade is. It's just that, unlike our asshole sibling, *you* didn't act on that attraction because you were committed to someone else—whether she deserved it or not." She put her hand on his arm and leaned against him, offering comfort.

"It's okay. I'm over Celia." He didn't want his sister worrying about him, and he rarely gave that bitch a thought anymore.

But Jade… He couldn't deny he was looking forward to seeing her again, though he'd never admit that to Holly, who tended to be a little *too* interested in his love life.

"Good. I'm glad seeing Jade won't be awkward for you. Because she's the event coordinator at the Meridian Hotel and I'm dying to get married there. I thought it would be better to see her in person instead of picking up the phone and saying, *Hi, this is Holly Matthews, your cheating ex-fiancé's sister.*" Holly shuddered. "Now, *that* would be uncomfortable." She wrinkled her nose in disgust. "But I always got along with Jade, so hopefully an in-person meeting will work out."

The line inched forward again, and they moved along with the crowd.

"There's no reason to worry," Knox assured her. "I'm sure Jade's a professional. I doubt she'll hold Theo's behavior against you."

Finally, almost twenty minutes later, they reached the registration booth, where they were handed their badges and information packets. Holly was a little wedding obsessed, and she'd brought a huge tote bag to fill with samples and brochures. Knox had a hunch, by the end of the day, he'd be carrying a heavy bag.

She took a few minutes to scan the map and mark

her targets before she grasped his arm and they were on their way. After an hour, he had to admit she knew what she was doing. She navigated the massive event hall like a pro, pausing at already crowded tables to pick up brochures, enter giveaways, and take business cards. The vendors she had real interest in, she paused to introduce herself, talk, and make an impression. He knew she'd been accumulating a mental list of who she wanted to follow up with. Hopefully, her fiancé would be the one to tag along to those upcoming meetings.

"This is Jade's booth," Holly said, pausing.

The corner location had no long table blocking it off from the people walking by. Instead, the entire space was open and carpeted, allowing for meet-and-greet conversations and making it extremely welcoming. High-top tables were strategically placed with brochures and bottles of water on each, providing a place for visitors to rest, and a young girl was busy replacing drinks and pamphlets on the tables after people left. Knox couldn't help but be impressed. Jade obviously had good business sense.

"I love the tulle backdrop with the fairy lights," Holly said, her brown eyes sparkling.

"It's beautiful." And so was the woman talking to clients.

Her pale blond hair was pulled into a loose braid that hung down her back, and the delicate features he remembered drew him in. As she talked, her hands waved expressively in the air, causing him to grin. Whatever they were discussing, it was obvious she loved her job.

Holly nudged his side. "It's good to see you smile."

He'd been thinking the same thing about Jade. She looked good. Happy. And he was glad.

"I told you that you liked her."

He rolled his eyes. "What are you, ten?"

Holly perched her hands on her hips. "Is it so bad that I want to see you happy?"

"No, but I know that gleam in your eye. You want to matchmake and that's where I draw the line."

"Yeah, yeah. Whatever you say," she muttered. But he knew nothing he said would deter Holly when she was on a mission.

He could handle his life, his choices, his women. *If* he decided to make a move on Jade, he didn't need his sister arranging things to his advantage.

"Do you want to go talk to her?" he asked.

Holly shook her head. "Not yet. I'll let her finish with those people first."

Knox nodded. Having Jade's full attention? He couldn't argue with that.

JADE DARE WRAPPED up her conversation with a

Jade ever wanted to think about—the family had closed ranks. Her older brothers, Asher, Harrison, and Zach, had painful memories of their birth mother. But Jade and her twin, Nick, had only been two when she'd left. They had no memory of anyone but Serenity as their mother, so that was what Nick and Jade called her. But Jade still worried about what her biological mother had done and what that meant for her own mental health.

"Speaking of men..." Lauren's voice broke into the morose thoughts Jade tried hard not to dwell on.

"We weren't." She narrowed her eyes at Lauren. "We were discussing my sister and, before that, Bridezilla."

Lauren opened a water bottle and took a sip. "Okay then. Just pretend we were discussing men. Are you still on a man fast? Because it's been a year and a half since you broke up with Dickhead, and I think it's time for you to get out there again." She twirled around and her long bob swung with her. "Mix and mingle. My neighbor invited me to go to a bar with some friends tonight. You should come with me." She turned pleading eyes on Jade.

Jade knew when she was being manipulated. Lauren had done it often enough during their college days at NYU, when she would try and get Jade to go somewhere she didn't want to go. Jade suffered from migraines and anxiety, and she was lucky that Lauren had stuck around, back in the days when partying was everything. A lot of Jade's high school friends had become bored with her *issues*.

"Thanks for the invite. I'll think about it."

Lauren raised an eyebrow. "You're lying."

Unable to hold it in, Jade burst out laughing. "You know me too well."

"Is it because of the man fast?" Lauren asked, her tone serious.

Jade took a quick glance at the rear of the exhibit, making sure Layla had gone back to her reading and wouldn't overhear their conversation. A man fast was what Jade was calling the time she was taking to fully get past what that lying, cheating SOB Theo Matthews, her former fiancé, had done to her. She considered it a necessity, something she had to do for herself before she moved on. After all, she'd jumped into a relationship too soon with Theo, after ending things with Douglas Webster, a creep who'd only wanted her for her family money.

If Mr. Right ever came her way, she wanted to be in the right frame of mind to recognize it. And so, taking the time to know herself first was imperative.

"I'd say I have good reason for steering clear of men," Jade muttered. "And would you stop saying those words? We're here to sell happily-ever-afters, not run people off," she said, tipping her head at the visitors looking at their brochures and photos.

Lauren sighed. "One of these days, you're going to give in and go out again. I just know it."

"Hi!" A perky redhead walked up to Jade and Lauren, ending their conversation, for which Jade was grateful.

"Hello," Jade said, smiling. "How can we help... Oh! Natalie! It's good to see you. I've talked to so many people today, I just dove in without realizing I already knew you."

The attractive woman laughed. "Six months and counting!" she said, her smile as big as her obvious excitement.

She was one of the brides Jade enjoyed talking to. "I know. You remember Lauren, right?"

"Of course!" Both women spoke at the same time and laughed.

"What are you doing here today?" They'd booked all her vendors already.

"John is having a guys-only day, so I figured I'd come sign up for some of the giveaways. I'm feeling lucky!" Natalie said.

"Well then, why don't you enter ours? We're offering a night in the bridal suite at the Meridian. You never know. You might end up staying there for free." Lauren winked at Jade and led Natalie toward the giveaway table, giving Jade a few minutes of blessed peace.

She picked up a bottle of water from a table, opened the cap, and took a long sip. As she replaced the top, a female voice called her name.

She put the bottle down and turned.

"Jade, hi!" Holly Matthews, her most recent ex's sister, rushed over and engulfed her in a hug. "I'm so happy to see you!" Holly exclaimed loudly in Jade's ear.

"Let her go, Holl," a deep, masculine voice said. "You're squeezing the life out of her." A rumbling *sexy* chuckle followed and she shivered at the sound.

Holly laughed and released her. "Sorry. It's just been way too long. I've missed you," she said, keeping Jade's focus on her.

Jade smiled. "I've missed you, too." She should have kept in touch with Theo's little sister. They weren't all that far apart in age and she'd always liked her. "What are you doing at the Bridal and Wedding Expo?"

"She's getting married," the same masculine voice said, drawing her attention and she glanced up, meeting Knox Sinclair's amused gaze.

He was Holly's brother, Theo's stepbrother, and the man whose wife Theo had slept with when he'd cheated on Jade. It wasn't a great connection to have, and they hadn't commiserated about it afterward. He was also the hottest man she'd ever seen, then and now. His appearance here was a surprise and butterflies immediately took up residence inside her. He was just that handsome.

"Hi, Knox," she said, trying to calm her heart rate at the sight of him.

"Jade." He tipped his head in greeting.

Her name on his lips sent tremors of awareness shooting through her. With his dark hair, hazel eyes that appeared more green than brown, and a face that was close to perfect, she couldn't help her attraction to him. He had a straight nose, a strong jaw, and full lips she'd imagined kissing. And yes, she'd felt guilty about it, since she'd been with Theo at the time. But she hadn't acted on the urge, which was more than she could say about her ex. Knowing she could study him now without guilt was liberating and she drank him in.

A football team owner, he always wore a sport jacket and slacks, looking imposing and put together. And more her type than Theo, the goalie for the New York Rockets, had been. She'd never dated an athlete before, but Theo, the hockey player, had been persistent, and she'd been anxious to jump back into the dating pool after her first broken engagement.

What a mistake that had been. Theo had taught her well—she had shitty taste in men, bad judgment, and had no business dating anyone, not even a guy as hot as Knox Sinclair.

"How are you?" she asked.

Even his genuine smile with straight white teeth drew her in. "I'm good. And you?"

"Busy." She gestured around the booth.

"Impressive display," he said, his gaze following her wave.

Pride filled her and she smiled. "Thanks. We worked hard." She looked to where Lauren had been, but her assistant had stepped to the side to talk to Holly. She hadn't realized she and Knox had been left alone.

"Why are you the one here with Holly?" she asked. Most brides brought their mothers, friends, or future husbands. Jade knew Holly's mom had passed away. "Where's the groom?"

"He's out of town. Holly asked me to come with her to check things out."

His indulgent tone when he spoke of his stepsister was so different than Theo's had been. Theo had had no patience for Holly, her bubbly personality, or her desire to please. And they were blood relatives. Looking back, Jade had ignored a lot of red flags when it came to Theo, and she wanted to kick herself for being so blind.

Knox tipped his head towards his sister and Jade

took that as a cue, walking over with Knox following.

"Holly! Your stepbrother just told me about your engagement. Congratulations," Jade said, joining Holly and Lauren.

"Thank you. I'm very happy," Holly said. "Look!" She held her out her hand to show off her ring.

Used to this with all her brides, Jade lifted Holly's fingers to admire the beautiful emerald-cut diamond. "Gorgeous. I'm thrilled for you."

"Thrilled enough to be my wedding coordinator and help me find a date at your hotel?" Holly clasped her hands together. "Please?"

Jade glanced at Lauren, who winced from behind Holly's back. "I'd really love to work with you, but we're booked for the next year. When did you have in mind?"

Holly glanced at Knox, who shrugged.

"Your call," he said. "What did you and Miles discuss?"

She bit down on her lower lip. "We figured a year, but I have to admit, I was hoping to find an opening sooner."

Jade wrapped an arm around Holly's shoulders. "It's difficult to plan a wedding on short notice, especially if you're looking for all the bells and whistles. How about you give me a call at work? I'll look at my calendar and check the soonest open date. In the meantime, why don't you sign up to win a free night in the Meridian bridal suite." She pointed to the sign-up area.

Holly, looking disappointed, nodded. "I guess I knew that. I was just hoping things would go my way. Can you let me know if you get a cancellation, though I know that's highly unlikely?"

"Of course. Leave your number with Lauren. If something opens up, I promise you'll be my first phone call." Jade didn't mention that, if something like that happened, it would mean that another bride-to-be was left devastated. Jade had been down that road herself, and just the thought of it made her ill.

"Hey! It's been so long since we've seen each other. Do you mind if I get a picture of all of us together?" Holly asked. When Jade nodded her agreement, Holly went into action. "Come on, move over here." Despite attendees walking in and out of the booth, Holly directed Jade and Lauren to stand in front of the fairy lights.

Knox stood to the side, his arms folded across his chest, his gaze on Jade, causing the awareness she already had of him to multiply.

"You, too, Knox! Come on." Holly grabbed his hand and pulled him across the floor. "Stand here." She nudged him between Jade and Lauren.

His broad shoulder rubbed against Jade's arm, and

her nipples puckered in reaction.

"I don't think it's necessary for me to be in the photo," Knox said, his voice gruffer than before. Had their touch affected him too?

She didn't want him to duck out so she touched his shoulder. "Stay. You'll be good PR for the hotel."

Holly nodded. "See? Now step back."

"I can take the picture," Layla offered, placing her book on a stool.

Holly smiled. "That would be great. I want to put it on my Instagram." She handed Jade's sister her cell phone.

"As long as we're doing this, can you make sure to get the hotel and business logo in the photo?" Jade gestured to the Meridian Hotel Events sign.

A few minutes and several photo attempts later, they had the money shot, and everyone was happy with the end result. Holly immediately posted the picture and tagged them all. Lauren walked across the booth to talk to a woman who'd been waiting patiently to ask a question, and Layla settled back onto her chair to read.

"Before we go, I want to enter the giveaway," Holly said. She stepped over to the table with the forms and filled out her entry.

Jade stood with Knox, and he looked away from Holly to meet her gaze. "How have you been?" he asked.

She assumed he was referring to getting past the heartbreak they'd both experienced. "I survived Theo, if that's what you're asking."

He shook his head. "That's not what I meant. How are *you*?" Those gorgeous hazel eyes studied her intently.

"I have work, friends, close family. I'm good," she answered honestly.

His smile warmed her. "I'm glad."

"All set." Holly joined them before she could ask how he'd been. "I'll be calling you to book when you're free… and to see if something opens up."

Jade nodded. "Sounds good. I've missed you," she said.

"Me, too." Holly tipped her head to the side. "Do you have dinner plans when the expo is over? We should all go out, right?" she asked, nudging Knox not too subtly with her elbow.

Jade bit the inside of her cheek. At this point, she was certain Holly was trying to push her together with Knox. Which would be as awkward as it sounded, and she assumed he felt the same way.

"Why not?" Knox surprised her by saying. "I'm free."

Holly's eyes lit up. "Jade?"

She hesitated but saw the sincerity and hope in

Holly's eyes. Since Knox also wanted to see her again, she decided one dinner couldn't hurt. "Sure. I should be able to make it around seven thirty, if that's okay? Somewhere mid to uptown would be easiest."

"Not a problem. Holly will make a reservation since it was her idea." His sexy lips turned up in a grin.

"How many people are we? Lauren, can you make it?" Holly asked.

"Sorry," Lauren said, as she joined them. "I have plans."

Jade wished her friend could be there to act as a buffer against Knox. The man's sex appeal was potent, and Jade would have appreciated Lauren's support in her battle against Holly's obvious matchmaking intentions. Then again, Lauren might hop on the set-Jade-and-Knox-up bandwagon.

"How about your sister?" Holly tipped her head toward Jade's quiet younger sibling.

Jade shook her head. "My parents are picking her up later this afternoon."

"So that makes three of us then. Great! We can all catch up. See you later!" Then Holly walked off, her attention on her phone, probably looking for reservations.

Knox tipped his head. "Later, Jade." He winked and strode off after his sister.

Jade tried not to drool as she watched him walk

away. Then she turned to her booth and got back to business. But even as she talked with prospective customers and handed out brochures, she looked forward to spending an evening with Knox and couldn't help wondering what she'd gotten herself into.

★　★　★

KNOX WAS IN a surprisingly good mood as he pulled out of the parking lot at the expo for the drive back into the city. Sure, Holly had manipulated him and Jade into dinner, but since it gave him an excuse to spend time with a pretty woman who intrigued him, he figured why the hell not go?

From the corner of his eye, he glanced at his sister. "You're looking pretty smug."

She turned to him. "About dinner? I am. About having to wait a year for the wedding? Not so much."

"If you want to get married sooner, pick a different venue. I know the upscale places book out early, but I'm sure we can find you somewhere you'll be happy."

She frowned. "That's my dream location."

"Then we'll just have to wait."

Her cell phone rang and she answered the call. "Theo! Guess where I just went?"

Knox shook his head. She'd never stop trying to get her brother interested in her life.

"Oh! You saw the picture I posted?" She listened to the asshole's answer. "Yes, I'm still with Knox." She narrowed her gaze and glanced his way.

He shrugged and merged onto the highway.

"Fine." She let out a groan. "Theo wants me to put him on speaker." She hit the button on her screen. "You're up," she said to Theo. "What's going on?"

"There are thousands of wedding planners in Manhattan. You don't need to use Jade," Theo said.

Knox set his jaw. What the fuck was Theo's problem? He was the one who screwed things up with his fiancée. It was none of his business if Holly wanted to work with Jade.

"I want to get married at the Meridian, and she's their wedding planner. Her family owns the hotel and she runs their entertainment. You know that," Holly said.

"A place is a place. Pick somewhere else. It'll be awkward for me." Theo's voice sounded more like a whine.

"This isn't about you." Knox was growing more pissed by the second. "It's about Holly. And she is the only one who gets a say."

He'd like to remind his stepbrother that Knox was the one paying for this wedding since *their* mother had disappeared with her latest wealthy pawn. Theo hadn't offered up a dime. But Knox would never make Holly feel bad.

"You're so full of shit, Knox. It's not about what Holly wants. You just want to be around Jade. You always did have a hard-on for her. Guess you like my leftovers," he said, chuckling, but Knox could hear the anger beneath the sound.

He forced out a deep breath and gripped the leather steering wheel harder. "Don't you have playoffs to prepare for? Or are you still working off your last suspension?" Knox couldn't help but deliberately goad his stepbrother. If something didn't go Theo's way on, or off, the ice, he made everybody miserable.

"At least I'm an athlete. You needed your daddy's inheritance to be any part of a team."

"Theo, cut it out," Holly said, the joy from the day leeched out of her voice.

It was time to end this conversation. "I'd say it's been a pleasure, but we both know that would be a lie." Knox glanced at Holly. "Disconnect the call."

Theo did the honors first and ended the conversation before she could hit the button on the phone.

"Sorry I let him push me into an argument," Knox told his sister. "But don't let him get to you. He's always been self-centered. He thinks everything's either about him or someone's done him wrong. None of this has anything to do with you."

Holly sighed. "I know. He never takes responsibility. Anytime something bad happens to him, it's someone else's fault." She picked at her nails. "I'm sorry for what he said to you."

Knox reached over and grasped her hand. "Don't take his shit on yourself. Come on. What happened to the smug, giddy woman who set her brother up tonight?"

Holly blinked in an exaggerated fashion. "Who, me?"

He laughed, glad her good mood had returned. "That's better. Now get to work finding us a restaurant."

She turned up the radio and began scrolling on her phone, giving Knox time to think about Theo's reaction. If a mere photo with Jade had set his stepbrother off, Knox could only imagine what Theo would do if Knox actually spent time with his stepbrother's ex. And unsurprisingly, he didn't care.

Chapter Two

THAT EVENING, JADE left the expo early. Lauren, the best assistant ever, had offered to run the booth until the event was over and even handle cleanup. Jade had apologized for saying no to Lauren's plans tonight and yes to Holly but Lauren had been giddy that Jade was going out... with Knox.

Without Jade having to say anything, Lauren understood that, with her migraines, Jade would be in sensory overload from the noise in the convention center. A nap before dinner would definitely help her recuperate for tonight. Lauren was a true friend and Jade owed her one.

Back at her apartment in Manhattan, she took a long shower, washing off the grime of the day. She dried her hair and settled into bed, hoping exhaustion from being on her feet all day would pull her into a deep sleep. It didn't.

She couldn't stop thinking about Knox Sinclair. He wasn't an easy man to put out of her mind. She'd always been a sucker for a man in a suit, and Knox, dressed in a sport jacket and white shirt, unbuttoned enough to show a sprinkling of chest hair, had made her mouth suddenly go dry.

But Jade wasn't breaking her man fast, not even for the sexy guy who had reappeared in her life. When a woman was betrayed as often as she'd been, she learned to be cautious, regardless of the chemistry. Still, she'd be a liar to deny the attraction. And if she wished she could unbutton that shirt and lick his chest? Nobody would ever know.

After twenty minutes of staring at her ceiling, she accepted she wouldn't be getting any sleep, but her ears were no longer ringing from the noise echoing around her. She got out of bed and walked to her closet. Picking out an outfit to wear for dinner with a man she didn't want to be tempted by wasn't easy. Still, her pride made her want to look good.

She took her time with her makeup and left her hair down.

She chose a new Milly designer dress, a one-piece black sleeveless mock turtleneck that ended with a Boho colorful handkerchief hem she adored. The shoulders were a generous cut, revealing arms she worked hard to keep toned. She paired the dress with a medium-height block heel and a fun natural-and-black-striped clutch that had a thin strap if she wanted to hang it over her shoulder.

Grabbing a short, thin black leather jacket, she was

ready to leave. She opened her ride share app and called for a car. Knowing she'd see Knox again, the butterflies in her stomach had only gotten worse, and by the time she stepped out of the car and walked into the restaurant, they'd fully taken flight.

At the hostess stand, the woman there informed her the rest of her party had already arrived, then led Jade to a back corner. Knox and Holly sat at a table, deep in conversation, giving Jade a chance to stare at Knox without his knowledge.

Once again wearing a sport coat—this one a tonal navy, with a light blue shirt beneath—he was everything she liked in a man. Dammit. Why couldn't he have worn a T-shirt? Maybe she wouldn't have been as attracted to him.

Liar.

As if he sensed her stare, Knox looked up and saw her, then rose to his feet. Had Theo ever stood up when she walked into a room? Ummm... No. His gaze slid over her like a soft caress, his warm smile telling her he liked what he saw. She let out a sigh. At least she wasn't alone in this unwanted attraction. Though he didn't seem to mind.

"Sorry I'm late," Jade said. "My Uber got stuck in traffic."

Holly waved her hand, dismissing Jade's concern. "We haven't been here long."

"Here. Have a seat." Ever the gentleman, Knox pulled out her chair and Jade sat down.

He settled in the chair next to her, making her aware of the alluring scent of his cologne—a scent any sane woman could get high on inhaling.

"Was your expo booth successful?" he asked.

She nodded. "It was," she said with a grin as she placed the folded napkin on her lap. "We accumulated a list of names to add to our mailing list. Some women even wanted to set up appointments to book wedding dates two years in advance."

"Two years!" Holly let out a squeak, causing Jade to laugh.

"I know, you're in a rush," Jade said. The young woman's enthusiasm was infectious.

Knox groaned. "She's determined," he muttered.

The waiter walked over and paused by Holly. "Can I get you something to drink?"

"I'll have a glass of pinot grigio."

When he looked at Jade, she said, "A club soda with lime, please."

"Sir?" he asked.

"Whiskey, on the rocks. Dirty Dare, if you have it." Knox locked eyes with Jade and winked.

Her panties grew damp at that subtle gesture, and she shifted in her seat.

"I thought Dirty Dare was vodka," Holly said as

the waiter walked away.

"It is. But they bought out a whiskey company last year," Knox said. "Right?"

Jade nodded. "We did." Her family vodka business, in which all her siblings had a stake, had begun to expand, buying a well-known brand and relabeling it under the Dirty Dare name. "To quote Asher," she said, using finger gestures, "*if we want to be a major player in distilled spirits, we need to invest in a variety of categories of alcohol.*" She indicated the end quote with her fingers and laughed. "No joke though, Asher is brilliant at what he does."

She admired her brother's business savvy. When he'd decided to create Dirty Dare Vodka, he'd insisted all the siblings contribute from their family-provided trust funds. He then proceeded to increase their income, ensuring none of them would ever have to worry about money. Each of them still worked in their chosen fields—Harrison was a world-famous, award-winning actor, Nick and Jade worked in the hotels, and Zach spent his hours in the bar he owned, though everyone suspected Zach did more than just run a bar. Her brother loved being mysterious.

"Asher's smart," Knox agreed.

"You and Asher are old friends, right?" Holly asked her brother. "I remember you mentioning him back when... Yeah, I remember." Her cheeks turned red. It was obvious she'd just realized that when she'd mentioned *back when*, she was talking about the time Theo had cheated on Jade with Knox's wife.

"They are," Jade murmured. She glanced at Knox. "Though I didn't realize Theo was your stepbrother until he and I started dating. It was a little... complicated in the end," she said.

"Incestuous but not," Knox grunted, just as the waiter set down their drinks.

"I was going to say it was just so wrong. Sometimes, I can't quite believe I'm related to Theo." Holly wrinkled her nose in disgust.

As if to change the subject, both Holly and Knox picked up their drinks and took a long sip. "Are you sure you don't want something stronger?" Holly asked her.

Jade chuckled. "I don't drink. I get migraines and I've found drinking just isn't worth the pain it'll cause."

Holly nodded in understanding. "I'm sorry. That was insensitive of me."

"Not at all. I get asked about it all the time. I'm good with club soda."

They paused to peruse their menus, and since Holly had chosen a steak restaurant, Jade ordered filet mignon and maple roasted Brussel sprouts, with bacon on the side. Knox chose a rib-eye, fries, and asparagus, and Holly, the glazed salmon. For the next hour, they talked about everyday things, their jobs, Holly's ideal wedding plans, and Jade told stories about some of the Bridezillas she'd had to contend with. They laughed, and Jade relaxed, allowing herself to enjoy both Holly's and Knox's company.

After dinner had been cleared, Holly placed her napkin on the table. "I hate to eat and run, but I have to go pick up Miles from the airport."

"You didn't mention that," Knox said, raising an eyebrow.

"Are you sure?" Holly leaned down and picked up her purse. "I could swear that I did."

Knox shook his head. "I'd remember," he said wryly. "We took a car share service here. How are you picking him up?"

"I'm meeting him at the airport. He left his car there, so stop with the twenty questions. You two stay for dessert. Thanks for dinner," Holly said, laughing, and kissed his cheek. "Bye, Jade. This was fun! We'll have to do it again soon. I'll be checking in about any cancellations, but don't forget to call me if you hear something!"

She waved and walked to the front of the restaurant in a flurry of activity Jade was coming to associate with Holly.

"That was a setup," Knox said, an amused smile

on his face.

"Definitely a setup." Jade couldn't help but laugh. "Your sister is one determined woman."

"That she is." Knox slid an arm over the back of his chair and leaned close. "What do you say we stay? We can have coffee and dessert *and* get to know each other better."

She shouldn't. She really shouldn't. But looking into his eyes, Jade couldn't think of a good reason to say no.

KNOX SHOULD HAVE been annoyed at his sister's machinations, but he was enjoying his time with Jade too much to worry about Holly's games. Her move, leaving him alone with Jade, was vintage sibling matchmaking, and Knox intended to make the most of the time Holly had given him. That didn't mean he wouldn't find a way for some payback. The next move was his.

"So? Dessert?" he asked, looking into Jade's gorgeous navy-colored eyes.

"That sounds perfect. Something decadent." She ran her tongue over her lower lip in an innocent gesture that had him taking notice. "What do *you* want?" she asked, and he barely withheld a groan.

He cleared his throat. "Lady's choice. We can

share."

"Sounds good."

The waiter brought over menus, and after looking through them, Jade ordered a concoction with vanilla ice cream, a strawberry and blueberry compote, and crushed graham crackers mixed in and on top.

Personally, Knox would have rather nibbled on the woman beside him, but when the dessert arrived, her eyes lit up, so he'd have to make do with food.

Since he had her undivided attention, he decided to take the opportunity to get to know her better. He leaned in close. "Why don't we get the obvious awkward subject out of the way for good? I know Holly already mentioned Theo, but you and I never talked—*afterwards.*"

"If we must." Jade wrinkled her nose, but her expression turned to delight as she closed her mouth over the spoon, slowly pulling out the utensil and licking it clean.

Jesus. His cock was rock hard, making him extremely uncomfortable. "Let's call it clearing the air. I'll go first. My stepbrother is a douchebag."

She laughed. "That he is and I'm well rid of him. As it turns out, I'm well rid of men in general."

"Ouch."

She grinned at his reaction.

"Why do you say that?" he asked.

She scooped another helping of dessert before meeting his gaze. "I doubt you know this, but I have two broken engagements behind me. Two." She motioned with the spoon for emphasis. "My track record leaves a lot to be desired. And, as I've discovered, so does my taste in men." She glanced at the sundae-styled glass sitting between them. "However, when it comes to dessert, I know what I'm doing."

She scooped up more of the ice cream and berries, holding out the full spoon for him to taste. Her gaze held his as he opened his mouth and closed it around the dessert, letting the rich, sweet, cool mixture coat his tongue.

She pulled the spoon back, removing it from between his lips. "Good?" she asked.

"Delicious." His body vibrated with need, and it wasn't for more dessert. The woman sitting beside him made his mouth water.

"Oops." She reached out and swept her delicate finger over his bottom lip, removing some vanilla ice cream before he could dart his tongue out for a lick. "Ice cream," she said in a husky voice.

"Want to tell me about the idiots who let you slip through their fingers?" he asked.

She smiled. "Well, winner number one was a guy I met at Starbucks. I was rushing to a meeting. I bumped into him and spilled my coffee on his suit.

The barista didn't put the top on right." She shrugged. "I apologized and insisted on taking his number so I could pay for the dry-cleaning. We went on a few dates. In the beginning, he said he wasn't interested in anything serious, but later claimed he couldn't help but fall for me. Unfortunately, what he'd fallen for was my family name and money." She let out a sad sigh that broke his heart.

"Asshole. How'd you find out?" he asked, wondering if he could find the bastard and break a bone or two.

"My brother Zach. He realized what was going on and approached my fiancé behind my back with a prenup in hand. Douglas, that's his name, refused to sign. In fact, he laughed in Zach's face and bragged that he had me wrapped up so tight I'd do anything for him. Zach broke his nose and told me the truth. I thought I loved him, when the truth was, I never knew him at all."

Knox covered her hand with his. "I'm sorry. I know what it's like to be wanted only for money and not for myself."

She nodded. "Thanks for admitting that."

"Did Zach really break his nose?" he asked.

She laughed and nodded. "He said nobody fucks with his family."

Knox wasn't surprised. He'd have done the same

thing if Holly had ever been in a similar situation.

"No trouble for Zach afterwards?" Knox asked.

She shook her head. "Nope. Douglas was too afraid of Zach to even meet with me so I could return the ring." She shrugged. "So I sold it and invested the money."

"Smart." He picked up his water and took a long sip.

"What about you? Did you get your ring back?" she asked.

He coughed as the drink went down wrong.

"Are you okay? I didn't mean to pry, but since I answered your personal questions, I figured you owed me some answers in return." Her lips twitched, lifting in a naughty grin.

Knox liked this girl's sass. He cleared his throat and waited until he was certain he could talk without choking. "Fair point," he said at last. "Okay, here goes. Celia kept her rings and I'm sure she sold them, too. But it's not the same situation. Celia cheated on me." Bitterness rose, along with the memories.

"With your stepbrother." Jade's expression turned sad. "Which brings up another question, since we're being so honest and everything."

"Go ahead."

She pushed the melting dessert aside. "Theo could have cheated on me with anyone. I mean, he probably did. But why did he choose your wife? That was the one thing I could never understand. You two were supposed to be family. Look how close you are with Holly."

"Theo can be charming—I'm sure that's the man you first met." Knox paused, gathering his thoughts. "But deep down, he's an insecure little boy." He leaned his elbows on the table and steepled his fingers. He'd given this question a lot of thought. "From the day Theo's mother married my father and they moved into our house, Theo was jealous of me. If something didn't come easily, he looked for someone else to blame. Very often, he chose me. That was ironic because sports were more his thing than mine, at least back then."

Jade blotted those sexy lips with her napkin and placed it on the table. "I've seen him in action," she murmured. "When he had a bad game, he'd blame everyone else—his teammates, the coaches... even a fan once." She shook her head. "He always had excuses, never taking accountability for anything he did."

"Exactly."

She tipped her head to the side, her eyes unfocused, as if remembering. "I remember the time the coach benched him for a whole period. He'd missed a save and blamed it on the defenseman screening him so he couldn't see the puck. Theo had been livid. Then again, so was the coach." She cleared her throat. "It became my job to soothe his anger so he didn't lose his position on the team."

Knox recalled that moment. Rumors were that the owner was thinking of sending Theo down to the farm team for a while, until his attitude improved.

Theo couldn't risk that. He'd told Knox that Jade Dare made him appear important. His engagement to her would make him look like a man willing to commit, on and off the ice, making changes the team's management would approve of. Jade brought him respectability with her family name.

Knox grimaced, remembering. Far be it for his brother to actually put in the work to make himself respectable. He looked up at the woman sitting beside him. Jade had obviously fallen for Theo, unaware of his true nature.

"It sucks that you had to deal with his behavior. Theo is a piece of work," Knox admitted. "He thinks things come easily to me. And yes, I worked for the team out of business school, and when Dad died, I inherited it. But I inherited a team that hadn't made the post-season in years. I've worked hard to build a championship organization." He shook his head in disgust, thinking of his brother. "It's always been a constant argument with him about how life is unfair.

The less often I see Theo, the better."

Her features grew soft with understanding. "And your wife? I mean ex-wife?"

He raised an eyebrow. Jade was digging deep, but then, he'd done the same. "Celia was different when we married. My dad had just passed away and I was in a bad way. She was there. But once she was exposed to having a lot of money, she changed. She wanted more. I tried to be available to her despite how busy I was between taking over the team and settling my father's estate. No amount of time together ever satisfied her. She wanted to be my focus all the time."

Jade twisted her lips. "It doesn't seem like she went about getting your attention in the best way—not if she wanted to keep you as her husband."

He rolled his eyes. "Yeah, well, that ship has sailed."

If Celia hadn't cheated, Knox would never have considered ending the marriage. He'd seen how his parents' divorce had hurt his father, and his dad had raised him alone until Theo and Holly's mother came along. Knox had been determined to make his marriage work, but infidelity was something he just couldn't overlook. It helped that, by the end, his heart hadn't been engaged for a long time.

He studied the woman beside him. She ran her finger over the rim of her water glass, deep in thought.

"What about you?" Knox asked. "Are you over Theo?"

She lifted her gaze, her eyes locking on his. "Are you kidding? I was over him the day I found out."

He leveled her with a knowing stare.

"Okay, fine." She held up both hands in submission. "It took a long time to get over the hurt, but I really believe it was the pain of being duped and cheated on that stayed with me. Not to mention, it reinforced the fact that I don't trust my judgment when it comes to people. Especially men."

He winced at her admission but she obviously believed it was the truth.

"Anyway, once again, my brother came to the rescue. Zach assured me that I'd dodged a bullet. And that, in short, is why I am on an official man fast."

Knox jumped on her statement. "What's a man fast?"

"I've decided that there's no place for a man in my life. I'm done with relationships."

"After what you've been through, I can understand that. And honestly, I can relate, too." But he *was* attracted to her.

She had an outgoing personality, which was always a turn-on for him, a curvy body he longed to touch with his hands and his mouth, and full lips he was dying to kiss.

"Jade," he said in a gruff voice meant to let her know things between them had taken a more sensual turn.

"Yes?" Her eyes were open wide.

"I'm not looking for a relationship, either." He picked up her hand and settled his thumb on the rapidly beating pulse in her wrist. "But I do want you."

Her lips parted and a small puff of air escaped. "But my man fast…" She said the words without any heat behind them.

He grinned. "Change the definition. You're now purging *relationships* from your life. That leaves wiggle room for many, many *other* things."

She widened her gaze, her eyes dancing with delight. "It does, doesn't it?"

Yeah, he liked this woman. "It means you can come home with me tonight and we can have some fun."

Her tempting tongue swept over her bottom lip again. "In your bed?"

He nodded, his fingers toying with her hand, his thumb pressing into her palm. "And out of it."

Her eyes dilated, a haze of desire washing over them. "No strings."

"None."

"Just one night?" she asked for confirmation, her voice firm.

He grinned because he'd already won. These negotiations were just foreplay. Damn, he loved an easy win—not that he considered Jade at all easy. Just well worth his time.

"One night only," he assured her. "Agreed?"

She leaned close, her lips inches from his. The scent of coconut aroused him more than any expensive perfume he'd ever smelled.

"Get the check, Mr. Sinclair. We have a deal."

NO SECOND THOUGHTS. Jade repeated the mantra as she accompanied Knox to the Uber he'd called to take them to his building. Her palms itched with the need to put her hands all over his muscular body, and the urge to kiss him and taste him for the first time was strong. So no apprehension, no changing her mind. She planned to enjoy tonight. Enjoy *him.*

Knox confirmed the address with the driver, an apartment building on the Upper East Side, a few blocks from hers. Her heart pounded hard, anticipation building inside her.

On the ride, Knox held her hand, running his thumb over the pulse point in her wrist. "Nervous?" he asked.

She let out a laugh. "Not nervous. It's just… I don't do this often." *Or ever.*

His smile put her at ease. "I never took you as a one-night-stand kind of woman."

"And yet, that's all this can be." She needed him to believe her intentions. Jade was the type of woman who usually couldn't have sex without her emotions eventually becoming involved. But knowing what this was, and wasn't, up-front should help.

"Because you're on a man fast." To his credit, he didn't sound like he was making fun of her.

She grinned. "That and I tend to fall easily," she admitted. "And there is *no way* I'm getting involved in another relationship. But one time should be safe enough."

His sexy grin had her heart kicking harder in her chest. "Who said anything about just one time?"

She caught the naughty look in his eyes, and her panties grew damp. "You know what I mean. Tonight only."

The car came to a stop and Knox nodded. "Don't worry, beautiful. We're on the same page."

Her stomach fluttered at the endearment. He opened the door and climbed out, extending his hand to help her out of the car.

Tension built inside her as they passed the doorman, who smiled at her and acknowledged Knox by name. They took the elevator to the penthouse, the ride seeming to take forever.

Flashes of the movie *Fifty Shades of Grey* passed through her mind, but Knox didn't push her against the wall and ravish her. And that was too bad—her body was hot and ready for his.

The doors opened and he pulled out his phone to scan, allowing him access. Then he extended his arm, indicating she should enter ahead of him. After stepping inside, she looked around his apartment, which was decorated professionally but with a heavy accent on the masculine feel. She loved the open space, and though she'd prefer lighter accent touches to the darker color scheme, the place was gorgeous.

"I love the decor," she said, taking in the far windows overlooking Manhattan at night and the mocha-colored sofa, which had a comfortable, beckoning look.

"Thanks. I pretty much got what I asked for." He glanced around the space, as if seeing it from her perspective.

"Which was?"

He shrugged. "Masculine and comfortable."

She laughed. "You sound like my brothers."

"Speaking of your brothers, I heard Nick's a father." Knox tipped his head, indicating she follow him, then led her through the large living room and over to the kitchen area, which was also open concept. "Can I get you something to drink?"

Even his gentlemanly qualities turned her on. "No, thank you." What had he asked her? Oh. Her twin. "Yes, Nick's the father of a bouncing six-year-old girl and his wife, Aurora, is pregnant again."

She grinned at the thought of Leah, an adorable spitfire Jade loved to spoil. "He and Aurora met up again at one of Harrison's movie premieres. It's a long story, but essentially, they had a one-night stand, no last names exchanged, when they were younger. He left and she had no way of finding him to let him know she was pregnant."

He shook his head. "Wow. Thank God for fate."

"I know. I can't imagine them not ever becoming a family." Her eyes misted when she thought about what her brother might have missed out on.

"Good for them. I'm glad." He placed his phone on the counter. "So, you don't want anything to drink. What do you want, Ms. Dare?" He began undoing the button on his cuffs, causing her mouth to go dry.

She'd already agreed to do this, so there was no reason to be shy. "You," she said, reaching for the first button on his shirt. "I want you." She undid his shirt, slowly revealing muscular, tanned skin, and a dark sprinkling of sexy chest hair.

She breathed and inhaled his musky male sent and nearly moaned as arousal washed over her. She laid her palms on his chest, leaned forward, and pressed her lips to his warm skin as she'd daydreamed about doing earlier.

A low growl sounded from his throat. Next thing she knew, he'd lifted her up, and she had to wrap her legs around his waist to hang on. She expected him to carry her into the bedroom, but instead, he walked her across the room and pressed her back against the cool glass window. Then finally, *finally*, his lips were on hers.

His tongue thrust into her mouth and devoured her, as if he was starving. His lips were warm, his breath minty. He must have picked up a candy on the way out of the restaurant, too. The flavor exploded on her tongue, but beneath the fresh flavor, she tasted the man. Everything that was Knox aroused her, and she wanted more.

She clasped her legs tighter, allowing her to feel the swell of his erection against her core and causing a rolling wave of desire to wash over her. She pushed her fingers through his thick hair and held him in place, kissing him back, taking what he gave and offering more.

She didn't know how long they stood there, lips locked, hips moving and shifting, their lower bodies grinding against each other, getting lost in not just any kiss. A spectacular, mind-blowing kiss she'd never forget.

In an impressive feat while holding her up, he lifted the loose, generous lower part of her dress, and air drifted across her bare legs. He slid his rough fingertips up her thighs until he slipped beneath her skimpy thong panties and immediately ran his fingers through the slick dampness of her sex.

She gripped his hair and moaned into his mouth. He didn't break contact and her lips felt bruised, but everything about this moment was worth it. He rubbed along her sex and her hips jerked harder against him. Then he ran those digits through her wetness and pushed one long finger inside her.

She jerked her head to the side and pulled in a deep, much needed breath. He pumped his finger in and out, and her inner walls clasped him tight. "Oh, God."

"You're so wet and ready. You like this, don't you?" he asked in a gruff voice as a second finger joined the first, filling her even more. "You need this." He picked up a steady rhythm. "Tell me."

"Yes. Yes, I like this. I need it." She squeezed his fingers, moaning at the delicious feelings soaring through her.

Then his thumb pressed on her clit and tweaked back and forth at the same time one long digit found a spot inside her no one had ever discovered before. Like a bolt of lightning, her orgasm rushed through her. He kept up the internal massage, and stars flashed behind her eyes. Waves rolled over her, until she fell limp against him, grateful for the window at her back, holding her up.

"How was that for a kiss?" he asked, his voice cocky, but she couldn't begrudge him the arrogance.

"I think you can do better." She laughed and he pinched her ass.

"Wise guy."

She grinned, enjoying him very much.

"Okay, beautiful. Bedroom time." He lowered her to the floor, but before she could get her bearings, he'd shifted and lifted her again, this time heading for his room.

If that orgasm was anything to go by, she had one hell of a night ahead of her.

Chapter Three

KNOX'S COCK WAS stiff and desire was riding him hard as he carried Jade into his room. He couldn't remember the last time he'd wanted a woman this badly. That first kiss? Hot and sweet and beyond anything he'd experienced before. That one kiss had changed everything in his brain. Then, feeling her convulse around his fingers had been hot as hell, and he wanted his dick inside her the next time she came.

He laid her down on the bed and stared into her hazy eyes. "Strip, baby," he said, shrugging off his open shirt and letting it fall. Then he continued to undress, not wasting any time.

"Bossy," she muttered, but she was smiling.

Her shoes hit the floor with a thud, and his cock reacted to the sound. She wriggled around his bed until she'd pulled her dress up her body and over her head, leaving her in a sexy black lace bra that allowed her breasts to spill over the top. Her panties had a damp spot from his earlier ministrations, and he groaned at the sight.

Once he was naked, it didn't take long for him to

divest her of those skimpy undergarments, although it wasn't easy with her skimming her hand over his straining erection as he undressed her.

He joined her on the bed and lay alongside her, his palm skimming her hip. Goose bumps rose on her soft skin, and her dusky nipples puckered under his gaze. He dipped his head and pulled one of those tempting buds between his lips and sucked hard. Her body jerked and her hand loosened its grip on his dick, which was just as well. He didn't want to come before they got to the good stuff.

He teased, sucked, and grazed her skin with his teeth until her hips jerked and she slid closer, rubbing her beautiful, naked body against his.

When he could take no more, he rolled and reached over to open his nightstand and pull out a condom.

She sat up and plucked the packet out of his hand. "Let me," she said in a husky voice.

She ripped open the foil, tossing it over the side of the bed. Her small hand gripped his cock, and he drew a harsh breath, breathing out slowly, determined to last.

She pinched the tip of the condom, then rolled the latex down and over his aching erection.

"There!" she said, sounding proud of herself.

He chuckled through gritted teeth and pushed her

back down on the bed. "Okay, you've had your fun. Now it's my turn." He straddled her and looked into her gorgeous face.

"What comes next won't be fun?" She deliberately batted her lashes, teasing him.

He shook his head and grinned. When was the last time he'd enjoyed a woman in bed for anything more than sex? *She* was entertaining and he intended to take advantage.

"Hands and knees, smart aleck," he said.

Her eyes opened wide, but she immediately scrambled to switch positions and do as he demanded. He rose to his knees and ran a hand down her back, over the bumps in her spine, and around one round cheek and then the other.

She trembled but remained in place, and he leaned over, lifting her hair that hung around her face. "You're gorgeous, Jade. I need you."

"Then what are you waiting for?"

He kissed her cheek and positioned himself, his cock ready. He slid a hand through her sex, finding her wet and ready for him, and his entire body throbbed in anticipation. He put one hand on her hip and used the other to guide himself to her entrance.

The moment he inched in a notch, she groaned and pushed back, sucking him inside her in a smooth glide he hadn't expected. Her slick body clasped him in heat and he saw stars.

"Jesus, Jade. Give a guy a little warning," he said, though he wasn't complaining.

She laughed and wriggled her ass. "Move, dammit."

Now she'd done it. Grinning, he slapped one pale cheek, pulled out, and slammed back in deep.

"Oh, God!" Her pussy spasmed, gripping him tighter, and he picked up his pace.

His cock demanded and she gave, as he pummeled in and out of her body. The rhythm sparked pure pleasure. Between her vocal sounds, the noises created by their slick bodies, and the pulsing of her core around him, he broke into a sweat and ground his teeth to keep from coming.

A sudden need rushed over him and he pulled out completely.

She moaned. "Knox, no."

He flipped her over and she stared up at him, wide-eyed. "I want to see your face." He brushed her hair off her flushed cheeks. "I need to look into your eyes," he said as he thrust back in hard.

She whimpered and drew up her legs. He pushed her knees back. "Don't move."

She gave him a short nod.

Certain she'd leave them in place, he braced his hands on either side of her head and let himself go. He thrust into her over and over, losing himself in her cries and the pleasure rushing through him, but never breaking the connection he'd sought.

His eyes remained locked with hers, and her gaze held steady as they climbed higher. He was strung so tight, it wasn't long before he felt a warning tingle rushing along his spine. His balls drew up tight. Knowing he couldn't hold off any longer, he slid his fingers between them, running one over her clit, rubbing until she began to come.

She stiffened beneath him and ground her body into his. "Knox, I'm... Oh, God. I'm coming." Her eyes lost focus and her body shuddered around him, triggering his release.

He came so hard he damn near lost consciousness as he pounded into her, then finally stilled, as he continued to fucking come.

Eventually he collapsed and immediately rolled over so as not to crush her. "Jesus." He laid a hand over his forehead as he did his best to come back to himself.

He turned his head and found her eyes closed, dark lashes fanned over her pale skin as she pulled in deep breaths. At the very least, he knew she'd come as hard as he had.

"Are you okay?" he managed to ask.

She turned and met his gaze. "I really don't know,"

she muttered, her cheeks flushed red. "That was intense."

It sure as hell was, he thought. "I hope that means it was good for you, too."

His wisecrack did the trick, and she burst out laughing, breaking the tension. Because that experience had shaken him as nothing else ever had.

He got up and walked to the bathroom to get rid of the condom and clean up, returning with a washcloth for Jade. Her cheeks remained a pretty pink, telling him that nothing about tonight had been in the realm of normal for her, either.

He tossed the small washcloth onto the nightstand and turned to pull her against him.

"I should go," she said softly.

Oh, hell no. He understood the need to run, and she'd made her intentions, or lack of them, clear. But so had he. "You promised me one night," he reminded her, then wrapped an arm around her waist and pulled her close. "And tonight isn't over yet."

He waited until her body softened against his, telling him he had his answer. She was staying. If one night was all she'd give him, he intended to make the most of it.

JADE WOKE UP, immediately aware of the fact that she

was in Knox's bed. It had been a night to remember. When he said it wouldn't *just be one time*, he hadn't been joking. She was sore in places she'd forgotten about and feeling muscles she hadn't known she had.

She glanced over to find his breaths coming deep and even. He was asleep, giving her the perfect opportunity to slip out unnoticed. As much as she'd enjoyed their time together, he was too sexy, too good in bed, and all too tempting. The only way for her to stick to her no-relationship rule was to leave before he woke up. Because this man was potent and made her want so much more than she was ready for.

She slid out of bed, collected her clothes, and made her way to the bathroom, where she washed up and did her best to run her fingers through her hair to tame the messy strands. It was bad enough she'd be doing the walk of shame in last night's clothing. She didn't need her wild hair announcing what she'd been up to.

She opened the bathroom door and tiptoed through the bedroom, hoping to find her purse in the outer area of the apartment. Although she felt guilty leaving him without saying goodbye, it was better this way. There'd be no uncomfortable conversation or awkward silences.

She made it to the bedroom door and was about to step into the hall when she heard his voice. "Going somewhere?"

She cringed and slowly turned toward him. "Good morning!" she said with a forced, bright smile.

"Is it? You're running like you have regrets." He'd pushed himself to a sitting position and was now studying her, his arms folded across his broad chest.

"No. Definitely not. I just thought it would be easier for both of us if I—"

"Made a quick getaway?" He raised an eyebrow. "Easier for you, maybe. But I'm not so difficult to handle. Stay and have breakfast before you go."

She paused. "Didn't we say one night?"

"And now it's morning." He swung his legs over the side of the bed and rose, standing there in all his naked glory.

As her gaze clung to parts of him she knew intimately, her mouth grew dry.

"Besides, I said breakfast, not more sex." Nonplussed, he strode to the dresser and pulled out a pair of sweats. "Although I wouldn't say no if you were in the mood for more sex."

She ignored his tempting statement and watched his gorgeous body move and bend as he pulled on the pants. "I'll stay for breakfast," she murmured.

His smile caused butterflies to take flight in her stomach again, but she ignored them, telling herself she enjoyed his company. Why not hang out with him a little longer? Besides, sneaking out had been a shitty thing to do. "I'm sorry I tried to run out on you."

"I get it." He walked over to where she remained in the doorway, his big body cornering her against the frame. "One-night stands are usually pretty awkward the morning after. But I'd like to think we're more than that."

"But we agreed—"

"On one night, I know. And I'm not going to pressure you. I just thought since we confided in each other, we're friends now. Right?"

She swallowed hard. Why did that one word disappoint her when she didn't want anything more? "Yes," she agreed. "We're friends."

"Then wait while I get ready. We'll go downstairs to the café on the corner and get breakfast. Then I'll hail you a taxi or call for an Uber."

She smiled. "I'd like that."

A little while later, they were sitting across from each other at a typical Manhattan diner. While Jade ordered a mushroom omelet, Knox chose the Hearty Man's Breakfast, a huge meal of scrambled eggs, pancakes, bacon, and sausage.

They'd been served their coffees, and both were taking a moment to savor their first sip of caffeine. "God, I needed this," she murmured.

He chuckled. "Long night?" he asked with a knowing grin.

Her cheeks heated and she was sure she flushed red. "Funny."

"Actually, I thought it was amazing." The gorgeous hazel eyes she'd been mesmerized by last night as he'd entered her now studied her intently.

"Me, too," she admitted.

"Amazing enough to do it again?" He lifted the white mug to his sensual lips, his gaze still steady on hers over the top of his mug.

Her belly twisted, desire flowing through her at the thought. But she needed to be strong and stick with the course she'd chosen. No men. No hurt.

She sighed. "Knox, we had an agreement."

He lowered the mug to the table. "Can't blame a guy for trying." He winked just as their breakfast was served.

They began to eat in companionable silence.

"No bacon or sausage?" he asked.

She shook her head. "The nitrites are bad for my migraines."

His gaze softened. "You really suffer with those, don't you?"

She nodded. "Ever since I was eight."

Jade clearly remembered overhearing her brothers talking about her mother's mental problems, how she couldn't take the pain, so she'd chosen death to escape it. So when Jade had started to get those same head-aches, too, she'd been terrified.

Jade vividly remembered lying in a dark room and Serenity taking care of her, bringing in cold cloths and putting them on her forehead. But she'd never let them get her down, always fought to get through the day to do what was on her schedule.

"I'm sorry," Knox said, interrupting thoughts she'd much rather not dwell on right now. "I hate that you have to deal with them."

She managed a smile. "They're something I've grown used to. I've learned how to push through, most days, though now and then, a migraine will prevent me from functioning." And then there was her anxiety.

Apparently, Theo hadn't shared much with his stepbrother, and Jade was glad for that. She didn't need Knox knowing all her flaws. Just one more reason not to get any further involved with this seemingly perfect man. Theo had been considerate of her in the beginning, too… until her migraines got in the way of his social life. He wasn't happy unless he was hanging out in loud bars, and she just couldn't take that for long.

Nor did she enjoy that kind of socializing. As much as she'd wanted to make her fiancé happy, she'd wanted them to make each other happy, too. And that meant not giving up who she was to please him. She'd often told him she didn't mind if he went alone. After all, she hadn't wanted to ruin his fun. Though she'd wished he'd do more of the things she enjoyed, too. Compromise. Something Theo didn't understand. And she hadn't expected his *fun* to be cheating on her. She was certain Knox's wife hadn't been Theo's only indiscretion.

"Hey. Where did you disappear to?" Knox asked as the server set the check on the table.

She shook her head. "Sorry. I was just lost in thought." Something she tended to do often. Serenity had always affectionately called her a daydreamer. Jade didn't mind. It was part of who she was.

Knox grabbed the check before she could, and when she reached for her bag, he shook his head. "I've got this."

He'd picked up the tab for dinner last night, too. "I can treat you to breakfast," she said.

"Call me old-fashioned but I want to take care of this." He pulled his credit card from his wallet and handed it to the passing server.

"Thank you." She smiled, appreciating the gesture.

While they waited, a feeling of disappointment settled over her, and she knew it was because it was soon time to say goodbye. Still, she believed she was doing the right thing.

A few minutes later, he'd signed the credit card statement, and they both rose from their seats.

"I can catch a taxi," she said as they stepped out the door and onto the sidewalk.

He held her hand and walked over to the curb. At the first sight of an empty cab, he raised his arm, hailing it.

The car crossed lanes and came to an abrupt stop, bringing her time with Knox to an end. He opened the back door, but when she moved to get in, he blocked her entrance. "What's your address?" he asked.

She told him and he bent down to repeat it to the driver.

Standing tall again, he clasped her waist in his hands and pulled her close. "It's been fun," he said in the gruff, rumbling voice she found so sexy.

"Very." She couldn't deny him the truth.

"Glad we're on the same page." He dipped his head and pressed his lips to hers, too briefly for her liking.

Then he stepped aside so she could get in the back of the taxi. "Goodbye, Jade," he said, his gaze holding hers as he shut the door, closing her inside.

"Goodbye, Knox," she choked, placing her palm on the window as the car pulled away.

JADE SAT AT her desk, poring over her calendar and events for the week. Mondays were always her day to make sure there would be no hiccups in her upcoming appointments and that she was prepared to handle any potential difficulty with the parties scheduled at the hotel. She had three event coordinators who worked beneath her, as well as Lauren. Together, they could handle anything.

Luckily for her, she'd worked day and night on Friday and Saturday this past weekend, giving her little time to think. Because when she had a free moment, memories of her night with Knox came rushing back. The man had magic hands, a skilled mouth and tongue, and a voice that could make her come just hearing that deep rumble alone. She shivered in her seat and her nipples puckered inside her bra. Dammit. The man didn't even have to be here for her to be all worked up.

Though she hadn't been able to get him out of her head, she had no regrets about their time together. He was just that hard to forget.

She tried to concentrate on her laptop screen but found it impossible. A sudden knock on her door was a welcome distraction. "Come in!" she called out.

Lauren sauntered into her office and plopped herself into a chair. "So, what are the odds that Holly will call by nine thirty a.m. today?" she asked.

Jade grinned. Knox's sister had called the office daily for the last week, hoping that someone had canceled their wedding, opening a slot for her sooner. She always followed up the question with a long assurance that she wasn't wishing a broken engagement on anyone. She just wanted to be married at the Meridian as soon as possible.

Jade glanced at the time on her screen. Nine fifteen. "Maybe she's learned to give people some time before calling in? I'll take ten a.m."

"No, she's too impatient to wait. But we'll see," Lauren said, laughing.

Jade grinned. "How was your weekend?" Although Jade had worked, overseeing two parties that her coordinators had handled, she'd given Lauren time off.

Her friend leaned back in the chair. "I had a date."

Jade raised an eyebrow. "Seriously? I didn't know you were seeing anyone."

"We matched on a dating app, and believe it or not, it went well. I'm seeing him again." Lauren's voice pitched with excitement.

"I'm happy for you." Lauren deserved to find a decent guy.

"Thanks." Lauren grew silent for too long, and Jade wondered what was going on in her friend's mind. "Okay, I have to ask. Why won't you see Knox again? If he was such a great way to end your fast, then why not see where it goes?" She tucked her brown hair behind one ear.

Jade blew out a long breath. "I've already explained that to you." After she'd confessed to spending the night with Knox, she'd told Lauren why it could only be one night.

"I know you've been hurt more than once. But you deserve a good man, and from what I can see, that's Knox Sinclair."

Jade frowned. "I appreciate that you want to see me happy. I want the same for you. But remember, I've screwed up twice. I'm not just on a man fast because I'm afraid of getting hurt, I also think my *man picker* is broken."

Lauren rolled her eyes. Before she could say another word, Jade's cell rang and she glanced at the screen. She used her phone for work, and sure enough, one of her brides was calling. Perfect, Jade thought. By the time the call was over, Lauren would have forgotten all about Jade's love life.

She picked up the phone and tapped the green button, putting the call on speaker since Lauren was working on this event, too. "Natalie, hi!"

"Hi, Jade." A loud sniff followed.

"Are you okay?" Jade asked, concerned by the husky sound of Natalie's voice. She glanced at Lauren, whose brows were scrunched in concern.

"No. The wedding is off. John said he can't go through with it. He isn't ready. He's not sure he loves me..." Her voice caught and she stopped talking. She blew her nose and hiccupped, obviously holding back sobs.

Jade had no doubt the tears were flowing, and her heart clenched in her chest. She'd been in Natalie's position and knew the pain. And sadly, she'd seen far too many other women go through the same thing. "Oh, honey. I'm so sorry."

"Thanks," Natalie whispered. "Can I get back to you another time to discuss details? I just wanted to tell you so you can rebook the venue."

Jade sighed. "Are you sure you don't want to wait a little while? See if you two work things out? Because if you cancel, there won't be an open date for another year, at least." She had to give Natalie the opportunity to hold on to the date. Just in case.

"No." Natalie's voice grew stronger, despite her pain. "I wouldn't take that bastard back if he begged."

"Okay. Call me when you're ready to talk." Money, deposits, and other logistics had to be discussed.

"I will. Bye." Natalie disconnected the call.

"Poor thing. She has a long haul ahead of her before she feels like herself again," Jade murmured. She glanced up to find Lauren staring at her. "What?" she asked.

"Are you okay?" Lauren's concern came through in her voice.

"I'm fine. This isn't about me. It's about Natalie." Jade didn't want to rehash her own disastrous engagements.

Lauren leaned forward. "It's also about Holly. Do you want to tell her she has a date in six months?"

Jade smiled. "Well, there's the silver lining."

Jade had taken Holly's number from the form she'd filled out at the wedding expo and had added it to her contacts.

"She's going to be so happy." Jade picked up her cell, found Holly's number, and hit send.

"Hello?" a familiar masculine voice asked. It was the same voice that sent tremors of awareness rippling over her skin.

"Knox?" she asked, confused.

"Jade?"

"Yes. I thought I was calling Holly. This is the number she put on the form she filled out at the expo."

His deep, rumbling laugh caused the body parts he'd awakened to sit up and take notice.

"Oh, this is perfect," Lauren said, grinning from ear to ear.

"Shut up!" She waved at her friend to be quiet.

"Excuse me?" Knox asked.

"Sorry, I wasn't talking to you," Jade said, feeling her cheeks burn.

"I think my sister was matchmaking by giving you my number," Knox said, sounding amused and not the least bit upset.

Jade pinched the bridge of her nose and opted not to acknowledge the point. "Can you give her a message for me?" she asked.

"Of course."

"We had a bride cancel her wedding on January eighteenth. I need Holly to let me know if she wants the date."

He let out a long whistle. "Well, that sucks for the bride, but I'm sure Holly will happily snatch that date up, even if it is the middle of winter. I'll let her know."

"Thank you," she murmured.

A long pause followed before he spoke. "How have you been?" he asked.

She envisioned him asking, his eyes sparkling with real interest.

"I've been good. Busy with work." *And thinking about you.* "How've you been?"

"The same. Working hard. Training camp is coming up in a few weeks. Getting ready for the season."

"So work, work, work. Sounds like my life in general." The honest words slipped out before she could stop them.

"Yet I remember how much fun you can be when you let yourself go." His innuendo was clear, as were the memories to which he referred. She squirmed in her seat.

He chuckled as if he could read her mind. "I plan to keep a close eye on the camp this year. I have big things planned." She heard him rub his hands together in anticipation.

She needed them to return to the point of this call. "So, you'll give Holly my message?"

"Of course I will."

"Thank you."

"You're welcome. And Jade? It was good talking to you. I'm sure I'll be seeing you again soon. Since you'll be working with my sister on her wedding, I mean."

"I'm sure you will," she said, the words coming out husky despite herself. The man was potent, even when he wasn't in the same room.

"Goodbye, Jade."

"Bye, Knox." She disconnected the call. Only then did she remember Lauren was still in the room, sitting there with one leg crossed on top of the other as she watched and listened, a smug grin on her face.

"No, you're not interested in him at all."

Jade narrowed her gaze on her best friend. "Shut up."

Lauren let out a laugh. "I'll go make a list of the

vendors we need to go over with Holly and leave you to salivate over your never-to-be-repeated one-night stand."

KNOX STARED AT his cell phone, unable to withhold a grin. Jade was so darned easy to fluster. And he had his sister to thank for their latest interaction. But that didn't mean he wouldn't give Holly shit for interfering in his life.

He pushed himself back from his desk, then walked out of his office and past his assistant.

Holly worked at the stadium in the PR Department, so he strode straight to her office. He knocked and waited for her to call out before he walked in.

"Hey, big brother."

He rolled his eyes—she had two *big brothers*.

"Hey to you, too, little manipulator."

She fluttered her lashes. "Whatever are you talking about?"

He walked to her desk and sat on the corner. "You giving Jade my cell phone number in case she needed to reach you?" He eyed her, unable to keep the smirk from his face. He never could stay angry with her for long. Not that he was angry. But she was fun to mess with.

"Jade called? What did she want?" Holly only cared

about the reason for the call, not what she'd done.

And that meant he could hold it over her until she admitted her meddling. So he shrugged. "She was so shocked to hear my voice, she almost couldn't remember why she was trying to reach you."

"Knox, come on! Tell me!"

"You first, little sis. Why are you playing games?"

Her brown eyes softened. "Because I love you and I want you to have a chance at happiness. I like Jade and so do you. Why shouldn't I try to help?"

He groaned and ran a hand through his hair. "I really want to be pissed at you."

"But you can't because I'm right." She leaned forward, resting her elbows on her desk. "Now tell me why Jade called!"

He smiled, despite her satisfied smirk. "You have a wedding date at the Meridian in six months if you want it."

Holly squealed, then got up and ran around her desk, squeezing him in a breath-stealing hug.

"I take it you want the date?" He peeled her off him and smiled at her excitement.

She nodded. "Of course. I'll call Jade back and see what happens next. I want to make sure none of the appointments are when you're out of town for your annual guys' weekend."

He'd forgotten all about his upcoming trip to Vegas. He and his business school friends got together once a year. But since his night with Jade, he'd been tied up in knots and wasn't focused on his schedule.

"Miles already said I should do whatever makes me happy. He's tied up with a merger, but he'll come to as many appointments as he can. The rest, you and I can handle, okay?"

"No problem," he told her.

"You do remember we have the FFT gala this weekend, right?" Holly asked. "The football team is giving away season tickets and you need to be there to represent the Warriors. It's for the Future Fast Track charity."

Shit. He'd forgotten. Although he had an assistant, Holly was more on top of his schedule than Olga, a new hire who hadn't yet proven herself up to the job, was.

"It's for a good cause. FFT helps kids aging out of foster care," Holly said, probably reading the annoyed expression on his face. Galas were no fun. "Not to mention, it's Aurora Kingston's charity. Actually, she's Aurora Dare now. She's married to Jade's twin, Nick. And that makes her Jade's sister-in-law." Holly nudged Knox in the side.

As if he needed her help in putting things together. "Jade will be there," he said, the event suddenly more appealing.

"The gala is at the Meridian, so I'm sure of it." Holly was obviously enjoying dragging this out.

He never knew where he had to be for a charity event until the day of the affair or, like now, when Holly gave him a heads-up in advance.

"There's been so much good news today," Holly said. "I'm going to call Jade. We have a lot to plan. It's a good thing I have your schedule," Holly said to him.

Her wedding planning would throw him and Jade together more often. And maybe, if he was charming enough, he could convince her that sharing another night together wouldn't hurt.

In fact, it would be fun.

Chapter Four

A LTHOUGH MOST OF Jade's job involved looking after weddings, she was also responsible for other events taking place at the hotel. And she was good at it. Still, the parties that involved her family were usually the most stressful and triggered her anxiety. A people pleaser by nature, Jade did her absolute best to make things perfect for those she loved. Thanks to her type A personality, she always strived for excellence... which often created a lot of unnecessary stress.

As she looked around the ballroom, set up for the FFT gala, Jade liked what she saw. The colors matched the charity's blue and silver logo. The silver chairs had been brought in special for the evening along with the navy tablecloths and silver napkins, keeping to the theme.

Yet she couldn't control her racing heart or sweaty palms and she hoped the loud noise of the band, the overhead lights and large crowd wouldn't trigger a migraine. She reminded herself that she'd been on a good migraine-free stretch lately, and she had no reason to believe that wouldn't continue. No matter what, she'd push through. She always did. She'd never miss something important to her family or bail early. Nor would she let her situation screw up a party at the hotel.

"Jade! Everything looks amazing!" Aurora Dare walked over to her. Dressed in a silver gown, which hung loose around the waist to accommodate her figure, Aurora was breathtaking. If Jade hadn't known her sister-in-law was pregnant, she never would have guessed. Though it was early, Aurora and Nick were thrilled to give their daughter, Leah, a sibling. And this time, Nick would be around for diaper duty.

Jade smiled at her sister-in-law. "I'm so glad you like it." Some of the tension in her stomach relaxed. "I hope you manage to raise a lot of money tonight. I didn't get a chance to check out all of the silent auction items, but I'm optimistic."

Aurora, her blond hair twisted into a sleek knot, was beaming. "It's going to smash all expectations. I just know it." Aurora had grown up in foster care herself, and aged out of it, before being discovered by the Kingstons as their long-lost sister. So this cause meant everything to Aurora. And therefore, it meant everything to the Kingstons, and to Jade and Nick's family as well.

"Where is Billie?" Jade asked of Aurora's assistant,

who was never far away. She was like a little fairy with her pink hair and outgoing personality. And from what Jade had seen, she was a very hard worker.

Aurora tipped her head toward the outer room with the silent auction items. "She's making sure everything is in place. She's already gone over the forms and starting bids ten times, but she's a perfectionist," Aurora said, smiling.

"Jade, a little crisis in the kitchen." Lauren walked up and joined them. "I'm sorry to interrupt. But you know that you have a special touch with Martin."

Jade shot Aurora an apologetic glance. "I have to go but don't worry. Martin has little tantrums now and then, but in the end, it's always fine."

"Jade." Aurora put a hand on Jade's forearm. "Relax. Nothing can ruin tonight. Even if all the sprinklers went off, we'd still make a ton of money." She winked and Jade's stomach relaxed.

This anxiety Jade experienced was a killer, but her sister-in-law had come to know her well in the last year, and she knew just what to say to ease her nervousness.

Jade managed a smile. "I appreciate that, but please stop jinxing things." She blew a kiss so as not to mess up Aurora's makeup and walked away, heading for the kitchen to deal with her temperamental chef.

After calming Martin and separating him from a

new employee who had upset his *chi*, she and Lauren stepped into a quiet space for a few minutes before the actual gala began.

"Are you okay?" Lauren asked.

Jade nodded. "I am. Things are normal. I think I'd worry more if Martin didn't pitch a fit before every event."

Lauren laughed. "Good. Then I should ask you if you're aware that Knox Sinclair is on the guest list?"

At the mention of his name, Jade's stomach did a somersault. "I noticed," she murmured.

But she'd immediately put it out of her mind—in order to get things ready for tonight, she'd had to. He hadn't mentioned it when they'd spoken about Holly, and Jade had too much on her plate to worry about seeing him again. *Liar.* In her downtime, she thought about nothing else. Not that she'd admit that to Lauren.

She bit down on the inside of her cheek and wondered if he'd be bringing a date. Her chest hurt at the thought and she gave herself a mental slap because he had every right to do what he wanted with whoever he wanted. She'd pushed him away. Now she'd worked herself up and needed to change the topic of conversation before Lauren pushed further.

"Did I mention you look beautiful?" Jade took in Lauren's sleek hair and gorgeous gold-beaded gown.

"I know what you're doing, but thank you, anyway. And you look beautiful, too. Knox will be blown away when he sees you." Before Jade could reply, Lauren's gaze slid beyond Jade to the ballroom. "I need to go check on something. Break a leg!" She winked and took off, leaving Jade to shake her head at her friend's antics.

What was with all the matchmakers in her life? Couldn't Holly and Lauren just leave well enough alone? Then again, maybe she wasn't being fair. Though she'd spoken to Holly a few times to schedule a cake tasting and some other things the young woman was eager to take care of early in the process, she hadn't mentioned tonight's event. So, it was just Lauren she'd have to watch.

Twenty minutes later, the first guests began to arrive. They checked in, received an auction brochure, and were given their table number for the dinner portion of the evening. The photographer hired for the event—who would be sending photos to the social media sites covering it—had arrived and had begun snapping pictures.

Deciding it was time to collect her family and move them into the main ballroom, she headed for the glass wall and bar at the back of the room. Aurora had found Nick and he'd wrapped an arm around her waist, pulling her close. Jade smiled at the sight of her twin, a wanderer who'd finally found his home with Aurora.

He stood with their playboy brother, Harrison, who still showed no signs of wanting to settle down. And beside him was Asher, who'd sworn he'd remain single forever. But for now, everyone was happy, and that was all that mattered. She joined them, nudging in between the guys.

"Hey!"

"Jade! I did a walk-through and couldn't believe this place. You've done a spectacular job. Congratulations," Asher said, lifting his glass in her honor.

"Told you," Aurora said. She took a sip of what looked like sparkling water.

Jade smiled, pleased and proud. "Thanks. I'm so glad we're all together. Are Mom and Dad here?"

"They are. Dad took Serenity to see the auction items," Asher said.

As the oldest, he'd been nine when their real mom left, and he'd been calling Serenity, their nanny, and later stepmom, by her first name his entire life. So had Harrison, who'd been six, and Zach, who'd been four but mimicked his older brothers. Only Jade and Nick called her Mom. Somehow, it all worked.

"Sorry to run, but I see an old friend. I'll meet you all inside the ballroom." Asher excused himself and walked across the room, meeting up with none other than Knox.

One look at him in a tuxedo and she was done for. If she thought he looked hot in a sport jacket, seeing the man in formal wear nearly bought her to her knees. Especially since she now knew what it felt like to push the dress shirt off his shoulders and press her lips to that sexy, muscular chest.

He caught her looking at him, and his smoldering gaze met hers. Those lips lifted in an alluring smile, even as he continued to talk to Asher. Still looking her way, he raised his whiskey glass, paused, and took a sip. She couldn't stop staring at his every gesture, finding each movement mesmerizing.

She heard her name being called and reluctantly turned away but not before acknowledging one pertinent fact. If he asked her to come home with him again, she'd find it impossible to say no.

KNOX WISHED HE'D been able to switch up the seating cards so he could be next to Jade during the long dinner and interminable speeches that followed the meal. Instead, Holly talked about her wedding options, and her fiancé, Miles, listened indulgently. At least Holly had picked a good man. Knox was comfortable with his sister's choice and felt confident she'd be happy with the attorney who hung on her every word. Her groom-to-be also knew how to interrupt her without being rude. And even Knox had to laugh at how smooth the guy's moves were, as he swept Holly off to the dance floor when he'd had enough talk of cake and color schemes.

Knox, on the other hand, would wait until closer to the end of the evening before making his move on the woman he wanted in his arms.

But it wouldn't hurt to get started. So he rose and strode across the room with one purpose in mind—to corner Jade, who'd been darting from person to person, making certain the important people tonight were happy, catering to Aurora and Sasha, who ran the charity… and avoiding Knox. He had no doubt he'd been unable to get a word with her because she was deliberately dodging him.

She wore a sleeveless floral gown in a mixture of blues that set off her unique indigo eyes. The deep V neckline plunged down both the front and back of the dress, revealing skin he wanted to run his tongue over and taste again. After he devoured those bright red lips, of course.

The hem of her dress pooled on the floor. With her sleek, straightened hair, she gave off a statuesque, regal impression. Any man would be proud to have her on his arm.

She stood beside a younger woman with pink hair,

and they appeared to be in deep conversation. Using her distraction to his advantage, he stepped up beside her and waited until they finished their talk.

"Thanks, Billie. I'm glad you and Aurora are happy with the turnout. I've been on top of everything. Let me know if there's anything else we can do for you."

"Will do." The young woman smiled and walked away.

Jade drew in a deep breath and let it out slowly, as if she needed to calm her nerves.

He stepped up behind her. "Anything I can do to help you relax?"

"Knox." Jade turned, her lips parted, and all he could think of was having that mouth wrapped around his cock.

Knowing it wasn't the time or the place for him to react to that thought, he slid a hand around her waist. "How about a dance?"

She shook her head. "I really should keep an eye on the party."

"You've been doing that all night."

"How would you know?" she asked.

He couldn't stop his grin. "Because I've been keeping an eye on you. Come on. The music just changed. You can fit in a slow dance with me." Without waiting for her to agree, he guided her toward the parquet floor in the center of the room.

"I really need to be working," she said as he eased her into his arms and they began to sway to the music.

If her actions or body movement had matched her words, he'd have let her go. But instead, she placed one hand in his and allowed him to lead her in their small area of the crowded floor.

"You look stunning," he said as they began to move.

Her cheeks took on a light flush. "Thank you. You're pretty handsome yourself in that tuxedo," she murmured, brushing a palm over his lapel.

"Good to know you still like what you see."

She'd started off stiff, but the longer they danced, the more her soft body molded to his, reminding him of how perfectly they fit together.

"How have you been?" he asked, swaying to the music.

"Same as last time we spoke. Work keeps me busy," she said, her cheek close to his so they could hear each other speak. "You?"

"The same. I've had lot of meetings with my coaches, watching film of potential starters for various positions. A lot of late nights."

She laughed. "I suppose we're two workaholics."

"Hey. I take time to have fun. In fact, I'm going to Vegas in a couple of weeks with my business school buddies."

"The one with Asher."

He nodded.

"Now that sounds fun," she said with a smile.

The couple behind them bumped into Jade, shoving her against Knox. He steadied her, pulling her to him and keeping her there.

"I've been setting up appointments for Holly. She wants to start early, and I think it's a good idea for her to meet with the vendors the couple who cancelled had already booked, since it will be hard to get anyone else at this late date. I'm hoping she'll be happy," Jade said.

He chuckled. "Now that she has her favorite hotel, she's flying high. I promise you, she won't be one of your Bridezillas."

She laughed. "Good to know."

They continued to move against each other, the music segueing from one slow song to another. Sometimes they talked, other times, they simply swayed in comfortable silence, but Jade made no move to leave, and he had no desire to let her go. Even when the photographer stopped them for a photo, she came right back into his arms.

"Oh, wow. People are leaving," Jade said, glancing around for the first time.

"We could get going, too." He stopped their movement and met her gaze. "Together."

"I—"

He placed a finger over her lips. "Don't overthink it, Jade. It's just one more night." He hoped there'd be more, but for now, he just wanted to ease her into spending more time with him.

Her tongue darted out, and she licked his finger, causing his dick to stand at attention.

He took that gesture as a definite *yes*. "Do you have to stick around for cleanup?" he asked, removing his hand.

She shook her head. "We have a crew for that. But I should talk to Aurora and Sasha before I leave and make sure they're satisfied with the night."

He glanced at the table where the Kingstons had been sitting. "I think they're long gone."

Her eyes opened wide, and she looked over at the empty table, checking for herself. "I guess I'll have to call them tomorrow."

"If either of them had needed you, they knew where you were." He tipped his head toward the center of the ballroom. "Don't get stressed out if nothing is wrong." He'd already begun to realize how seriously she took everything in her life, and he admired her work ethic.

She nodded. "You have a point." She slid that tongue over her lips. "Umm, I reserved a hotel room for the night. It was easier to dress here and sleep over since the night would end late."

He hadn't expected her to say yes so easily, let alone invite him to her room upstairs. "Is that an invitation?" he asked, just to be sure.

She lifted her chin and nodded. "It's a quicker trip than to either of our apartments."

"Let's go, beautiful." He leaned close and whispered in her ear. "I can't wait to taste every inch of your skin."

A visible tremor rippled through her, and her eyes dilated with need. "I need to grab my purse."

He followed her to her table, and she retrieved her bag. Then he took her hand, leading her out of the ballroom and straight to the elevators. He wanted her in his arms—and his cock buried deep inside her body—as soon as possible.

THE ELEVATOR DOORS closed behind them before another couple could slip inside. Then Jade realized Knox was holding the *close door* button, preventing them from having company for the car ride to her room.

She let out a laugh as she pressed the button for the top floor. "You're bad. I bet other people are tired and want to get to their rooms."

"They can get their own damned elevator." He

pulled her against him. "I want to be alone with you."

This was why she'd agreed to another night so easily. He was so open about wanting her. He made her feel good about herself and being with him. Unlike her previous partners, who only focused on themselves, Knox paid attention to her, and she loved it. But she didn't want to lead him on or make him think she'd changed her mind about relationships.

"This is just one more night, right?" she said, wrapping her arms around his neck.

"Right. Just one more time. Now relax and enjoy." He pressed his lips to hers and slid his tongue inside her mouth. He tasted like whiskey and Knox and everything good. She rubbed her breasts against his chest as the elevator dinged and the doors opened on her floor.

He grabbed her hand. "Which way?"

They stepped into the hall, and she pulled her hand from his to open her purse and find her key card. "Left." They walked to her room and she let them inside.

No sooner had the door closed than the undressing began. She tossed her bag onto the outer suite sofa and sat down to remove her shoes. By the time she managed the little things women had to do but men didn't, he'd already stripped naked.

She stared, unable to take her gaze off his glorious

body. He was tanned and muscular and his cock stood erect, beckoning to her.

He walked over and held out a hand but she had other ideas. Sliding off the couch, she dropped to her knees.

"Jade, you don't have to—"

She gripped his thickness in her hand, shutting him up fast. Then she ran her palm up and down the smooth yet impossibly hard flesh. "Shh… I want to."

"Then I have to admit, I've been thinking about having those red lips around my cock all night." The words came out sounding more like a rumble of need.

Her panties grew damp at the admission, but it wasn't her turn yet. Leaning forward, she swiped her tongue over the head, tasting his salty essence. She teased him with a few more licks before wrapping her lips around him and pulling him inside her mouth.

He thrust once and she gripped him tighter, using her saliva to glide her hand up and down his shaft, her mouth following along with the movement. She was by no means an expert and had never enjoyed doing this before, but something about Knox was different. *She* felt different with him.

He wrapped his hand around her hair and used his grip to hold her in place while thrusting his hips back and forth, his thick erection gliding in and out of her mouth. At times, she wasn't sure she could take it, but as if he sensed her distress, he'd slow down and pull out, giving her time to catch her breath. Then he'd start up again.

Before she knew it, he released his grip on her hair. "I'm going to come."

She took the warning and ignored it, sucking him harder until he began to spurt in her mouth and down her throat.

Afterwards, he helped her to her feet and kissed her long and hard. "You just rocked my world."

She grinned and spoke honestly. "My pleasure."

"Now it's your turn." He stepped around her and unzipped the back of her dress. It easily slipped off her shoulders and down to the floor.

The dress had enough material to prevent her from needing a bra, leaving her dressed in only a dainty thong.

He spun her around and gazed at her, hunger in his eyes. "Jesus."

Before she could react, he dipped his head and pulled one nipple into his mouth and sucked, gliding his tongue, then his teeth, over the already hardened peak. He created a direct line from her breasts to her sex, and she trembled where she stood.

"All night, I watched you, wanting to taste your skin." He laved his way up, nuzzling her chest, arousing her with every swipe of his tongue.

Her hips began to rock, circling of their own accord. She felt empty, her sex pulsing with need as he suckled her neck and tugged on her earlobe—places she would never have thought were erogenous zones—making her wet and leaving her wanting.

Unable to bear it, she slid her hand between her thighs and rubbed her finger over her clit. But he grabbed her wrist, stopping the movement. "If anyone is going to make you come, it's me." His low growl was as insistent as the words, and she immediately removed her hand.

He picked her up and carried her into the bedroom, setting her down at the edge of the bed, her legs dangling over the sides. Then he lowered himself to his knees and spread her legs with his hands.

Her heart slammed against her chest as he parted her folds and swiped up with his tongue. She shut her eyes and arched her hips, lost in sensation. He didn't let up, licking and suckling on her sex until she was rocking her hips and grinding herself against his mouth.

He devoured her with an expert touch, his finger sliding into her, first one, then another, at the same time he pulled her clit into his mouth. She was already primed and ready from the heady high of making him come. It didn't take long for her to begin the climb, quickly peak, and fall over.

She'd barely come to herself when she heard the crinkling of a condom wrapper and forced her eyelids open. "Do you always keep one on you?" she couldn't help but ask, though she was grateful. She hadn't thought to bring protection with her tonight.

"I knew you'd be here. Can't blame a guy for being optimistic." He met her gaze, waiting for her reply.

She released the breath she'd been holding. "When you put it like that…" She couldn't remain tense or uncertain. "I didn't mean to make things awkward."

His expression softened and he leaned over her. "We may not be in a relationship, but while you're the one on my mind, I won't sleep with anyone else."

Without giving her the chance to say anything, he leaned down and captured her mouth. He plunged his tongue inside, and she was eager and ready, kissing him back. He'd already lined up his cock at her entrance, and as the kiss heated up, he thrust into her, filling her completely.

If she'd thought their first time together had been an aberration, she now knew she was wrong. Together, they were perfection, and their bodies moved effortlessly in sync. He had the ability to make her feel things no man ever had. The words he said, the things he did, the way he moved inside her… This was special. Whatever this thing between them was, he'd marked her for good. No one would ever live up to his memory.

"Hey, beautiful. Come back to me." He slowed inside her, waiting for her to open her eyes and refocus on him. "Where'd you go?" he asked.

"Where you took me." She cupped his face in her hands. "Make me come," she said.

And that's exactly what he did. By the time she fell asleep, she'd had her third climax of the night.

The man was addictive. And that could be a potential problem.

KNOX WOKE UP, hoping to pull a willing woman into his arms. Instead, when he reached over, he only found cool sheets. Pushing himself into a sitting position, he looked around the hotel room. Jade was standing across the room, wearing a sexy bra and panties, and rummaging through her suitcase.

"No morning cuddles?" he asked.

She turned, her gaze zeroing in on his bare chest. She shook her head sighed. "I have a family thing and I overslept."

She'd obviously showered, because her hair was damp and pulled into a messy bun and she had a light coating of makeup on her face, blush on her cheeks, and sparkling gloss on her kissable lips. She reached into her suitcase and removed a peach silk camisole and pulled it over her head, then went back for a pair of black leggings.

"I was hoping we could have breakfast together." Before they went their separate ways again. He wanted to get to know her better, to dig deeper than she'd let him in so far.

As she pulled on her leggings, she shot him a look filled with regret. "Breakfast is my family thing. Since we all stayed at the hotel, we're meeting in a private dining room."

He debated on whether to hide his disappointment and fall back on their one-night-only agreement—which he was coming to hate more and more—and decided to hell with it.

He patted the bed. "Come over here."

She hesitated, then stepped over and sat down beside him. He braced a hand on her thigh. "We're good together, Jade."

She stiffened but he kept his hand on her leg, keeping her in place.

"What's got you spooked?"

She opened, then closed her mouth again. "I wish I had time to talk but…"

"Family."

She nodded.

He understood commitments and released his grip. "I'll be seeing you at Holly's appointments this week?"

"Yes." Her lips lifted in a smile.

"I look forward to it."

She leaned over and brushed his mouth with hers. "Me, too."

Knowing that was as good as he was going to get from her for now and considering it was more than he'd expected, he leaned against the headboard, a grin on his face.

She slipped on a pair of shoes, grabbed a sweater, and headed for the door. She paused and glanced over her shoulder. "Bye, Knox."

He raked his gaze over her, wishing they'd had more time.

"Goodbye, Jade."

JADE SLIPPED INTO the elevator and leaned against the side, catching a glimpse of herself and the stupid grin on her face in the mirrored walls. She didn't recognize the reflection staring back at her. When was the last time she'd been this happy? Really, truly smiling when she was alone, filled with joy? She shook her head, shocked by the realization that it had been Knox who'd caused this euphoric feeling.

But as the elevator moved down the floors, she remembered that she couldn't be caught *glowing* by her family. They'd figure out the reason and start peppering her with questions. It took some work, but by the time the door opened, she thought she had her expression under control.

As she stepped out of the elevator, she ran into her twin. "Nick!"

"I was just coming up to get you." He swung an arm around her shoulders and led her to the small dining room. "It's not like you to be late. What kept you?" he asked.

She glanced at him in time to catch a smirk on his face, and she narrowed her gaze.

"More like *who* kept her." Harrison rose as she walked in, his curious gaze on hers.

She froze. "What is that supposed to mean?"

"Give your sister a break," their father, Michael, said.

"You and Knox?" Asher raised his eyebrows. "Isn't he a little old for you?"

She rolled her eyes. "That's none of your business. But how would any of you know?" As far as she was aware, her family had already gone to their rooms when she and Knox left the party last night.

"Aurora left her sweater on her seat. I passed you in the hall but you only had eyes for each other," Nick said, nudging her in the ribs like only a sibling would.

"And you told two friends, and they told two friends, and so on?" she asked, glancing around the table at her large family.

The triplets, Jade's brothers from Serenity and her father, were nineteen years old and home from college for the summer. They sat at one end of the table. And Layla, Jade's youngest sister, was texting on her phone, ignoring everything around her. But Jade's older, overprotective siblings were looking at her, waiting for answers.

They knew she'd left with Knox last night. And they knew she was late because they'd been together. Heat rushed to her cheeks but she refused to play their game.

"Nobody needed to tell anyone. There was media coverage about the charity auction, and there was an Instagram photo of the owner of the New York Warriors dancing with his stepbrother's former fiancée on Page Six online." Asher's eyes blazed with anger. "I don't know why they have to add gossip to the photo."

"Because that's their job," Jade muttered. As a Dare and the head of events at the hotel, she was often photographed and no longer let it bother her when she showed up in any form of media. "I've learned to ignore those kinds of things. You should, too."

"Come on, Jade. Sit here and let's talk about how great a job you did last night," Aurora said. She was sweet, trying to take the spotlight off of Jade's affair, or whatever it was.

Grateful, Jade walked over and sat down beside her sister-in-law.

"Why didn't you bring your boyfriend to breakfast?" Nick asked as he sat on Aurora's other side, leaving a chair between them. Their daughter, Leah, must be around here somewhere. At this point, Jade wasn't sure who was missing.

Aurora reached over and shoved Nick in the shoulder. "Would you leave your sister alone?"

"I'm serious, Jade. I want to talk to you about Knox. As much as I like the guy, the social media site has a point. You *were* engaged to his stepbrother," Asher said, as if she needed the reminder again.

She folded her arms across her chest. "And? Look, Knox and I have an agreement. We know what this thing between us is… and what it isn't. You don't get a vote."

Serenity chuckled. "She's got a point."

"Quit ganging up on Jade. She's an adult," her father said. "Besides, I don't want visuals of any of my kids *that way*."

Now Jade's cheeks were burning.

Zach, who she hadn't realized was missing, chose that moment to stroll into the room. With his leather jacket hanging from one finger, and wearing sunglasses, he glanced around the room. "Morning, family."

"How about we grill Zach about why he's late?" Jade suggested.

"How about not?" Asher shot her a serious look that told her they weren't finished with this discussion.

"What'd I miss?" he asked, pulling out an empty chair beside Asher and taking a seat.

"Nothing," everyone said at the same time, including Jade.

"Sorry we took so long." Mellie, Aurora's pseudo-mom, walked in, holding Leah's hand. "*Someone* splashed water all over her shirt, then stood in front of the hand dryer for way too long."

The adorable six-year-old grinned. "But I'm dry now!"

"Yes, you are," Jade said, grinning. "Come sit with Aunt Jade for a few minutes and tell me what's going on with you." Jade enjoyed Leah's chatter, but she couldn't deny she also wanted to distract her siblings from talking about her love life.

Leah rushed over and pulled an extra chair closer to Jade. "I have a boyfriend!" she said loudly.

And *that* took the focus off Jade for the rest of the meal.

Chapter Five

KNOX SHOWERED IN Jade's hotel room but had no choice but to put on last night's clothes. He called the gift shop downstairs and had a T-shirt sent up to the room so he wouldn't have to walk through the hotel in total formalwear.

After leaving the room, he stopped at the coffee shop in the hotel and ordered a coffee and an egg wrap to go, then he grabbed a taxi outside the hotel, gave the driver the address to his apartment, and sat back to enjoy his breakfast.

After spending last night with Jade and hearing her admit this morning that she was looking forward to seeing him again, Knox was in a good mood—even if the only time he would catch a glimpse of her was while they planned his sister's wedding. Although he was happily paying, he wished Holly had had her mom to help her make decisions on things like flowers and cake. But Holly's mother, Addison, was off with some guy in Palm Springs. Maybe it was guy number two or three by now. He only knew Holly deserved a mother who cared. Unfortunately, all she had was Knox. Even

Theo, her brother by blood, didn't give a shit about anyone except himself.

Knox's cell rang as he let himself into his penthouse. A glance at the screen had him groaning.

Knowing he couldn't put the caller off forever, he answered. "Theo. To what do I owe the pleasure?" The last time he'd heard from the prick had been the day Holly posted the photo of the two of them with Jade at the wedding expo, and Theo had laid into him.

"Dammit, Knox. Why Jade? Are you just trying to prove a point? That you can take her away from me like I took Celia away from you?" Theo asked, sounding even more pissed than the last time.

Knox couldn't help but let out a laugh. "You're kidding, right? Jade dumped your ass over a year ago. What we do now has nothing to do with you. Just like nothing about my life ever has... *asshole,*" he muttered more to himself than his stepbrother.

"I heard that."

"And I don't give a shit."

"How do you think I felt waking up to find a photo of you and my ex on Page Six? Do you have any idea how many tags I got? People ragging on me? I told you to stay away from Jade," Theo said, his anger barely controlled.

"And I told you I don't answer to you." Knox disconnected the call, then dumped his tuxedo jacket and shirt on a chair.

He placed the phone on the nightstand and plugged it in, then sat down on the bed. Bracing his hands on the back of his neck, he stared up at the ceiling, wondering what the hell was going on with Theo.

His brother was a lowlife piece of shit who only cared about himself, but still, his attitude worried Knox. If Theo's focus was on Jade and not the playoffs, he'd never make it to the end of the season unscathed. And considering the fights he'd started on the ice and the sloppy way he'd played this season, Knox had no doubt his stepbrother was high on the Rockets' trade list. And if he lost his position on the New York team, there was no telling who Theo would blame or what he'd do.

Knox hoped Jade wasn't upset by the photograph taken of them. He'd have to check on her later, after her breakfast with her family.

His doorbell rang and he stood with a groan. "Now what?" Anyone who his doorman let up was on his approved list. Ted would call up before allowing anyone else past.

Which left Holly.

So he went to the door, expecting to see his sister. Not his ex-wife.

Beautiful in a cold, too perfect kind of way, Celia,

with blond hair and icy blue eyes, was striking. Too bad there was no soul, no warmth behind the façade. He wished he'd seen it sooner and saved himself a lot of heartache.

"Celia. How did you get past the doorman?"

She placed a hand on the doorframe. "Ted always had a soft spot for me."

"Poor sap can't see past your beautiful face to the bitch beneath."

She winced. "That's cruel, Knox, but I understand. I hurt you. But time has passed and I was hoping we could talk."

More like she'd seen the photo of him and Jade and, for some reason he couldn't fathom, was jealous.

She leaned forward, exposing her generous cleavage that did nothing for him anymore. "Let me in, baby. We can talk about the good times we had. I'll remind you," she said, her voice deep and husky as she reached out to stroke his face.

"I don't seem to remember any of those good times, actually." He jerked away from her touch. "We have nothing to talk about. I've moved on. You should do the same." He had no doubt she already had. This was a last-ditch effort to soothe her ego.

She withdrew her hand and clasped her fingers together in front of her. "I'm going to find a way to make it up to you."

"Please don't."

She ignored him, and her gaze lingered on his, making him uncomfortable. "Goodbye, Celia."

He closed the door without waiting to see if she walked away. And the first thing he did was pick up his phone and call down to the front desk. "Ted? Knox Sinclair. I'm going to give you the benefit of the doubt this time and ask you to remove my ex-wife's name from my visitors' list. If any unwanted visitors get by you again, though, I'll be calling the management company. Do we understand each other?"

"Yes, Mr. Sinclair. It won't happen again," the man said, sounding shaken.

Knox disconnected the call and blew out a long breath. Thanks to Theo's phone call and Celia's visit, he was wired. He changed into workout clothes and walked to the gym he frequented. Many of his business associates frequented it, too, but he hoped he didn't run into anyone he knew today. He needed to expend some energy and rid himself of the restless feeling that was suffocating him, not make small talk.

For the next couple of hours, he worked out, running the gamut from cardio on the treadmill to lifting weights. He used a trainer two days a week, but today, all he wanted to do was sweat out the demons that had followed him home.

By the time he was ready to head out, he was more

relaxed and his head was back where he needed it to be—thinking about Jade and figuring out how to get to know her better.

Falling into bed with her every time they ran into each other only worked if he wanted a fuck buddy. But from Jade, he desired more. He zipped his bag and picked it up from the bench, ready to go home. Instead, he found himself face-to-face with Asher Dare. From the man's frown and his everyday clothes, Knox could tell he wasn't there to work out, though this was his gym, too.

No, Knox knew why Asher was here. It seemed to be the day for confrontations. In this case, though, playing dumb worked better for him. "What are you doing here?"

"Looking for you. I called your cell, tried your apartment. Your doorman said you left in gym clothes."

The doorman had no idea what privacy meant.

"Well, it's good to see you again," Knox said. He and Asher had talked last night, before his dance with Jade.

"You might not think so after we talk."

And here we go, Knox thought. "Okay, let me have it."

"What would you do if I was sleeping with your little sister?" Asher lowered himself onto the bench in the locker room.

Knox joined him, appreciating the fact that Asher had taken things down a notch by sitting and not posturing or getting in his face. They were friends, after all.

He'd been prepared to defend himself, but suddenly, he understood where his friend was coming from. "I get it. And the first time, we agreed it would be just once, but…"

"It's happened before?" Asher raised his voice, and another man who'd come around the corner turned and walked away.

Shit. Knox hadn't meant to give Asher any more information than he already had. "Here's the deal." He ran a hand through his still-damp hair. "I like Jade. More than that, I respect her."

"You do realize she's seven years younger than you?"

"And twenty-six isn't an adult? Come on. You know she can make her own decisions." He sat with his arms on his thighs, looking over at a still-scowling Asher.

"We've always looked out for Jade. It's not that she can't take care of herself, she's just… more fragile than most people."

Sensing Asher had more to say, Knox waited.

"When our mom left, she was two. Technically,

Serenity is the only mother she knows. But when she got older, Dad had to tell her that our birth mother killed herself. Not long after that, Jade started getting severe migraines, and anxiety followed a few years later."

Knox held up his hand. He knew about the migraines, not about Jade's anxiety. But anything more he learned, he didn't want it coming from Asher. "Listen. What I was about to tell you before is that Jade is the one who keeps pushing for one night. Not me. I want to get to know her better. I'm not just hooking up with your sister. I'm respecting her wishes while trying to get past some pretty high walls."

"Your douchebag stepbrother did a number on her self-esteem. So did Asshole Number One."

Knox knew Asher was referring to Jade's first fiancé.

"She doesn't trust herself to make good decisions when it comes to men. And frankly, I only want her to be with someone I know will take care of her."

Knox raised an eyebrow. Jade could take care of herself, that much he knew. But he understood what Asher was getting at. "I'm not going to hurt her. I'd have thought you knew me better than that."

Asher frowned. "I still don't like this."

"Then it's a good thing you don't have to." Knox slapped Asher on the back. "Your sister is a grown woman. But if it makes you feel better, I can promise you, she's in good hands."

Hands that were dying to touch her again… but not before he learned what made her tick.

Asher grumbled but acknowledged Knox's point with a nod. Since he'd calmed Asher down, they went for a drink at a place near the gym and talked about Asher's Dirty Dare Vodka expansion into whiskey and other spirits. His friend tried to find out the Warriors plans for the season, but Knox kept mum. He trusted his friend, but he had to protect his team from eavesdroppers and potential leaks.

By the time they parted ways, Knox felt like Asher had calmed down about his sister, the friendship between the two men had been saved, and Knox could set his attention back on Jade.

JADE HAD HER hands full. Holly wasn't a Bridezilla, but she was a very hands-on bride to be. Lauren had given her a list of places the bride who'd cancelled her wedding had hired for her event, because they knew those vendors would be available. They'd already been in contact with the florist, baker, caterer, etc. to let them know they'd have to meet with a new client and the choices would be different. Holly wanted those appointments scheduled immediately.

Jade and Lauren did their best to accommodate her timeframe. She'd specifically asked for Jade to accompany her to the cake-tasting on Tuesday, and she'd agreed. Lauren was meeting with a new bride and her mother, and they hadn't cared who their initial appointment was with.

Jade glanced around her office, grateful for the window view. The sun was shining, the sky was blue, and fluffy white clouds filled the sky. She smiled. Today was a good day. The even barometer ensured her headaches would remain at bay and her anxiety was under control. She knew there was a deeper reason for her good mood, but she didn't want to delve too deeply into the sweet messages Knox had been sending her each night since she'd left him Sunday morning.

Lauren stepped into the doorway. "Knock knock." She smiled and walked into the room. "Someone looks happy."

"I was just admiring the view."

Lauren settled into the chair across from Jade's desk. "Are you sure you don't want me to handle the cake tasting, and you can meet with the potential bride?"

Jade shook her head. "Holly requested me, and you have the presentation down to a science. I'm not worried."

"Is that the reason? Or are you secretly hoping Knox shows up with his sister today?" Lauren drummed her fingers on the arms of the chair and grinned.

"I'm pretty sure Holly and her fiancé are the only ones coming. She wants him to be part of the decision." And Knox hadn't said anything about seeing her today when he'd sent his ten-p.m. *goodnight, beautiful. Sweet dreams* text last night.

She'd told Lauren about leaving with him last Saturday night, but nobody knew they'd been exchanging texts every night since. Although Jade usually replied with a simple *you, too* and a cute little sleep emoji with a 𝒵𝒵𝒵 beside the tired yellow face, or something along that line, the short interactions made her feel special. And she wanted to keep those messages to herself.

"So why that dreamy look on your face?" Lauren asked.

That was the problem with working with your best friend. It was hard to keep a secret. Before Jade could offer an answer Lauren would believe, Jade's office phone rang.

Her administrative assistant, Nancy, had already gone out for lunch, so Jade picked up the phone. "Hello, this is Jade Dare at Meridian Hotel Events. How can I help you?"

"Jade."

The familiar voice caused an immediate rush of shock and anger to rush through her. "Theo, why are you calling me at work?"

Lauren sat up straight in her chair.

"Because you blocked my number on your cell, and I have no other way to reach you."

She blinked in surprise. "Why would you even want to?" She gripped the receiver tightly in her hand.

"Because I know what game you're playing, and I'm warning you to stop."

"Game?" She had no idea what he was talking about but wasn't about to ask. She didn't want to be on the phone with him a second longer than she had to be.

"You're trying to make me jealous by cozying up to my brother and making sure there are social media pictures for me to see. I didn't think you had it in you to play the revenge game."

Jade opened her mouth and closed it again, unable to find the words to reply to his preposterous assumption. Finally, she formulated a reply. "Jesus, Theo. Not everything I do is about you. In fact, nothing I do is about you anymore." Her heart pounded hard in her chest, and the anxiety she'd been so proud of keeping at bay came thundering back.

"So you aren't staging those photographs with Knox just to piss me off?" He scoffed as if she were a liar. "Please. I'm not that naïve."

"Apparently, you are." She let out a laugh she couldn't control.

"What's so funny?" Theo asked, clearly angry.

"I'm not doing anything. Trust me, I'm not allowing my picture to be taken with Knox just to piss you off. Just like I'm not sleeping with him to get revenge. I promise, you're the last person on either of our minds. Goodbye, Theo."

When he started yelling, she disconnected the call. "Oops," she said to Lauren, meeting her friend's startled gaze.

"Wow. You told him." Lauren began to clap, applauding her. "What the hell did he want?"

Jade placed her hand over her chest, aware of her pulse racing. She took a deep breath to calm herself. "He's not happy I'm spending time with Knox. He actually accused me of having the photos taken and posted on purpose to make him jealous or to get back at him for cheating on me."

It wasn't in her nature to hurt someone on purpose—and she hadn't meant to be so blunt about her relationship, or whatever it was, with Knox—but Theo deserved that... and more.

"Asshole. Like he has a say in what you do."

Jade shook her head. "I'm just in shock that he even cares at this late date."

Lauren glanced at the phone she held in her hand. "I wish we had time to go for lunch and discuss this in detail, but we have appointments to get to. Promise me a girls' night soon?"

Jade smiled. "You got it. How about this weekend?"

"I have a date on Friday night. How's Saturday night?" Lauren asked.

Jade admired her friend's ability to put herself out there by dating strangers. "New guy?"

Lauren nodded. "Last one ghosted me."

Jade frowned. "Okay then. Saturday night is perfect." She pushed her chair back and rose to her feet. "I'm going to the ladies' room to freshen up and head out. I'll talk to you this afternoon. Good luck with your appointment."

"Same to you."

A short time later, Jade stepped out of the Uber she'd taken to the bakery where she was meeting Holly for the cake tasting. Despite feeling like she'd finally gotten the upper hand with Theo, she couldn't seem to calm her nerves. Her confrontation with him had brought on the stomach churning she hated, along with a dull throb on one side of her head. Ignoring how she felt, she walked inside to do her job.

Holly didn't need her to choose flavors—those were personal preference. As for cake style, Holly had promised to bring photos of what she had in mind so they could collaborate on keeping with the general colors of navy and cream.

She stepped into the showroom, expecting to see Holly and meet her groom-to-be, Miles. But Holly had brought her brother along, as well. The young couple sat looking through an album of cakes, while Emmaline, the owner, baker, and creator, spoke to Knox. Holly and Miles looked up, waved, then returned to their perusal of cake pictures.

Knox and Emmaline both turned her way. Emmaline, always Jade's first choice for any event that needed a cake, rushed over to give Jade a hug.

"Hi, Emmaline! It's so good to see you." Jade embraced her in return.

She stepped back and glanced at Knox. "You're a surprise." A handsome one, wearing a sport jacket she wanted to peel off him so she could bury her face in his chest and inhale his masculine scent.

Emmaline stepped away, looking at Holly and Miles over her shoulder. Knox stepped closer and leaned forward.

"A good one, I hope." Jade expected his lips to brush her cheek. Instead, he'd whispered in her ear, causing her to tremble.

"Come see!" Holly's voice had her stepping back and reminding herself to act more professional.

She cleared her throat, took a deep breath, then walked over to the happy couple. For the next two hours, they tasted samples, listened to Emmaline describe what flavors went well together, and discussed the shape and type of cake they wanted. For someone so certain of her wedding venue, Holly kept changing her mind on the various elements of the cake. Miles mostly left the final decision up to Holly. Which meant, at the end of two hours, she was still waffling.

Though it was Jade's job to keep the bride calm and facilitate her choices, today had been a rough one for her. Her headache, which had started as a slight pounding, had turned into a full-blown migraine. She just needed to wrap things up here and she could go home, take her meds, grab an ice pack, and fall into bed.

"You don't have to make the final choice today," Emmaline said. "You can get back to me. Take some time and think about it."

Yes, Jade thought. "That sounds like a good idea."

"No." Knox shook his head. Until now, he'd been quiet, letting the couple taste and discuss their options. "It's a cake. It's going to be beautiful, you'll be so busy you'll barely taste it, and everything today was delicious. You can't go wrong. So choose."

He folded his arms across his chest, but despite his

firmness with his sister, he appeared more frazzled than when he'd arrived. His hair was messy from running his hands through it, and he'd undone a button on his shirt when the room had grown warm.

Holly looked at him with wide eyes. "The almond cake with almond cream and white chocolate buttercream," she blurted out.

Knox shot Jade a pleased, full-of-himself smile. "There. Done."

"Thank you!" Holly jumped out of her chair and wrapped her arms around his neck.

He chuckled. "When Holly was younger, her indecisive nature became pretty obvious. So I'd force her to choose, and she'd always blurt out what she hadn't been able to commit to."

"And I was always happy," she said.

Knox looked at Miles, who appeared a bit dumbfounded. "You're going to have to pick up the slack on that," he told his future brother-in-law, grinning.

Holly glanced at her fiancé. "And you liked the almond?"

"We already pulled out the ones I didn't love. I just want you to be happy," Miles said, getting up and pulling her into his arms. "I already took the afternoon off. Let's go celebrate," he added.

Aww. These were the moments that made Jade love her job.

Emmaline smiled and wished the happy couple well. Then she turned to Jade. "I have to run. I have another. See you next time. I'll send you all the information, itemized." She glanced at Knox. "Nice to meet you, Mr. Sinclair. Thank you for your help."

Emmaline walked out the door, and Jade drew a deep breath, letting it out slowly. She braced her hands on the table and sighed. She hoped she could make it home without getting sick.

JESUS. THE LAST two hours had felt longer than two entire days, Knox thought. He always had patience when it came to his sister, but she'd severely tested its limits today. He glanced at Jade, who'd seemed to wilt as the day went on. She'd been easygoing and kind to Holly, but from the glazed look in her eyes and her flushed cheeks, something was wrong.

Relieved they were alone, Knox walked over to where Jade stood, hands clasped on the table, head dipped low. He slid a hand beneath her hair and cupped her neck, finding the muscles stiff and unyielding. He massaged them with his fingers, pressing into her skin and moving in slow circles.

She let out a moan that went straight to his cock. "What's wrong?"

"What isn't?" she asked, causing his movements to

still.

"Keep going. Please," she said.

"Then talk to me."

"Keep doing that, and I will." She hadn't moved and waited, head down.

He began to knead her muscles once more. "I have a migraine," she murmured. "It started earlier, along with my anxiety. I'm pretty sure you didn't know about that. Anyway, I'd hoped it would ease. After all, this was just cake tasting."

"But this afternoon wasn't very relaxing, was it?" He kneaded her neck, moving his thumbs into the base of her scalp.

"Who knew your sister could be so indecisive?" She let out a small laugh. "But it wasn't her fault. I didn't have any medication on me. I've felt good for so long, I forgot to make sure I had it when I switched bags."

"What triggered it this time? Do you know?" he asked, moving his thumbs higher.

She hesitated.

He leaned close to her ear, inhaling the warm co-conut scent of her hair and ignoring his body's reaction, given how much pain she seemed to be in. "You can tell me."

"You're not going to like it," she said.

He had to remind himself to keep up the pressure

on her neck and head. "Tell me."

"It's Theo."

"What?"

"Theo. He called me before I left to come here." Her muscles stiffened as she spoke. "I'd blocked his number, so he called me at work."

Knox stopped moving his hands and turned her to face him, doing his best to stay calm for Jade's sake. "What did he want?"

She drew in a deep breath and let it out slowly. "He accused me of playing games, of deliberately staging photos to get revenge."

That stupid son of a bitch. "What did you say?"

Her hazy eyes met his. "First, I told him that not everything was about him... And then I added that nothing *I* did was ever about him."

Knox let out a chuckle. "I'd have liked to see his face. Is that all?"

Her cheeks grew a heavy shade of pink as she blushed and glanced away.

"Now I'm curious." He lifted her chin with his hand, forcing her to look him in the eyes.

She bit down on her lower lip. "I might have told him I wasn't having pictures taken with you to piss him off any more than I was sleeping with you to get revenge."

He stared at her in disbelief, shocked she'd go that

far. And then he started to laugh, because she'd shoved their relationship in his brother's face, and damn if the bastard hadn't deserved it after cheating on Jade with Knox's wife. "You're my kind of girl, Jade Dare."

"You don't care that I told him?"

"Shout it from the rooftops. It's fine with me." He leaned in and brushed his lips over hers. Before she could react, he slipped his hand in hers. "Now, I'm going to take you home so you can get into bed and do whatever it is you need to in order to get rid of that migraine. Then we'll talk some more."

She blinked up at him, and he waited. "Are you going to fight me for trying to take care of you?" he asked.

"I'm in too much pain to argue. I could use your help."

He knew what it cost her to admit she needed him and was determined to show her that he wouldn't let her down.

Chapter Six

IT TOOK WAY too long to get from the bakery to Jade's apartment. Her head pounded, and she was frustrated with herself for not having brought her medication with her. It was just more proof that she couldn't take any sort of break from migraines for granted.

Luckily, Knox had driven his SUV, a BMW X5 with a shiny steel-gray exterior and a plush leather dark gray interior. The vehicle was so comfortable Jade was able to curl into herself and try to relax. But calming down was difficult when her heart was pounding in time with her head, and she felt as if she could feel the blood rushing through her body. The combination of migraine and anxiety had her getting worse. She white-knuckled the door handle the entire ride home. Every bump sent a throbbing pain shooting through her skull.

Knox was astute enough to remain silent as she sat with her eyes closed, breathing in and out. He finally pulled the car into a spot in front of her building. Apparently, the man had luck as well as charm and good looks.

With one arm around her waist, he helped her into the building. Once they were inside her apartment, he directed her to the bedroom, ignoring her protests.

"I'll get you whatever you need. Just get undressed, get comfortable, and climb into bed," he said.

She frowned at his bossy tone yet was relieved someone was here to help her. The last time she'd had someone to care for her was when she lived at home with her parents. Theo had been too preoccupied with his career to have patience for her *issues*, and her first fiancé hadn't been much better. Just thinking about that now, Jade had to wonder yet again about the choices she'd made and why she'd stayed with them for so long.

"Jade? I asked what I can get you?" Knox placed a hand on her back and she refocused on him.

"Sorry. I spaced out." Turning, she met his worried gaze. "I have ice packs in the freezer. Would you mind grabbing them? I'll get something to wrap them in when I pull out a T-shirt to change into. My meds are in my drawer, so maybe some water, too?"

He touched her cheek and nodded. "Change and lie down," he murmured.

She knew better than to nod. Instead, she gave him a small smile before he walked out of her bedroom. She pulled down the shades so the sunlight didn't make her feel like an ice pick was chipping away at her eyes and made her way to the bathroom.

By the time she'd washed up, changed into a soft T-shirt, pulled out her meds, and crawled into bed, Knox was waiting for her. He'd put a glass of water on her nightstand and had two ice packs in his hands.

She climbed into bed, picked up her medication, and swallowed it down. Then she wrapped the ice packs in soft cotton shirts to keep her head from feeling too cold and lay down, placing one pack beneath her neck and the other on top of her head. Eyes closed, she tried not to think about the pounding. It would take time for the edge to ease off the pain. The only positive thing about this experience was that this migraine hadn't come with nausea.

She was surprised when she felt the bed dip. Without looking, she knew Knox had joined her, stretching out alongside her. He shocked her more when he edged closer and wrapped an arm around her body, pulling her close.

He felt good. His strength, warmth, and very presence soothed her. "Thanks for staying."

"I wouldn't leave you alone and in pain. When you take the ice packs off, I can massage your temples if that'll help."

She sighed. "I don't know. Let's see how I feel in a bit."

"What can I do to help?" he asked.

"Talk to me?" His low voice calmed her.

"Sure. How about we get to know each other a little better? I know. Why don't I tell you something about me barely anyone knows? Then you'll do the same." He rubbed her arm in soft circles.

"Okay." Small talk would help her focus on something other than the pain.

"Hmm. Let me think." He paused and silence surrounded them. "I've got it. I wasn't athletic as a kid. My father owned one of New York's NFL teams and his son was a math nerd."

"You're kidding?" Nerd wasn't a word she'd have ever used to describe Knox.

"I wish. The kids used to make fun of me, so I became determined to learn everything I could about football. It was easy, since stats and understanding plays came naturally to me. And because the coach usually kissed my dad's ass every chance he got, he let me hang out with the team during practice." He let out a low chuckle at the memory. "I asked question after question, until I drove the man insane. But I learned fast. Soon I was helping to write winning plays."

That, she could see. "So the football players what? Adopted you? Made you their mascot?"

"You could say that. They also taught me how to work out, lift weights, and bulk up."

"So I have your old football player buddies to thank for your body?"

"Are you admitting that you like my muscles?"

She liked more than just that about him. "Quit fishing for compliments," she said with a smile.

"Okay, your turn. Tell me something about you that nobody else knows."

She pursed her lips in thought. "Well, my family knows this but nobody else does. Not even Lauren." But she thought she could trust Knox with this secret.

"I'm listening."

She drew a deep breath. "Jade isn't my real name. Well, it's my middle name. I was born Emery Jade Dare." It was something she tried to forget, along with other painful memories.

"Why do you go by Jade then? Do you just like it better?" he asked, his voice low in her ear.

She shook her head. Big mistake. The throbbing intensified and she moaned.

"Shh. Stay still." He pulled the ice pack off the top of her head and began to massage her forehead and temples.

She let his hands work their magic and she began to talk. "My mother chose the name Emery. My dad chose Jade. My father told me that one day, thinking it would help me feel connected to her, even though she was gone."

His hand stilled. "Did it? Make you feel closer to your mom?"

"Keep massaging, please." He began to rub her temples again and she forced herself to remain quiet until she could manage the pain. "I didn't *want* to feel connected to my mother. I was… I still am angry at her." For abandoning her and her brothers. For not loving them enough to get better. "After I found out, I made everyone call me Jade, and once I turned eighteen, I changed my name legally."

Her father had resisted for a while, but she'd been insistent. Finally, he'd given in, using the only name she would answer to.

"Asher told me your mother had mental health issues," Knox said quietly.

"She did. She had a desperate need for the attention she received when she was pregnant. Believe it or not, it's a real disorder people suffer from. The problem was, she didn't want to be a parent or take care of the kids she had. So Dad hired Serenity as our nanny."

"And you were lucky to have her," he said.

"Yes." She yawned, thanking God that the medication was starting to kick in. Her head was still bad, but now, she was getting sleepy. "I know it sounds selfish to be angry at someone for things they had no control over, but I can't help how I feel. She didn't stick around. She didn't try to get better, to be a real mother."

Knox stopped massaging and pulled her into his arms. "It isn't selfish. You had every right to want your mother to *be* your mother."

"Thank you for that," she murmured. In addition to the anger and hurt, she harbored guilt for her feelings. "I don't know what my father's deal was in allowing her to keep getting pregnant, and I don't want to know. That was between them. But as far as I'm concerned, Serenity is my mother."

Knox held her tighter. "Thank you for sharing."

She breathed in deep, inhaling his comforting scent, and snuggled closer to his warmth. Thanks to the medication she'd taken, she was finally tired enough to sleep. With luck, when she woke up, she'd be past the worst of the headache.

KNOX HAD LISTENED to Jade's secret, surprised she'd opened herself up to him. No doubt the pain had lowered her defenses, and though he didn't want her to suffer, he was grateful for the insight into the little girl she'd been. As the only female in a family of brothers, she'd have needed her mother as she grew up. Knowing she'd had Serenity in her life would have helped, but deep down, she still felt abandoned by the woman who'd given birth to her.

Knox didn't fault Jade for holding on to her pain, but he doubted the mixture of guilt and anger she was keeping inside her helped with the migraine headaches or her anxiety. He admired how hard she fought to do her job and live her life despite the potentially debilitating issues. She was a strong woman.

He waited until she'd fallen into a deep sleep, her breathing even and rhythmic, before climbing out of bed. There was a certain peace he found lying beside her, knowing he'd taken care of her the best he could. As much as he'd like to have pulled her into his arms again and felt her against him, it was still a workday. He glanced at her again and walked out of her room.

He stepped into the living area of her apartment and settled onto a large cream-colored sofa with soft pale-yellow pillows. The sofa was extremely comfortable and he leaned back as he worked. He called his office and checked in with his staff. He also spoke with Asher, confirming he and Knox's other friends were taking his plane on Thursday to Vegas, and made sure his assistant had his hotel suite booked for the long weekend.

Assuming Jade would wake up hungry, he ordered dinner, hoping she was in the mood for Italian. He chose a variety of entrees, knowing she could use the leftovers for the rest of the week. With everything on his agenda taken care of, he settled in to wait for her to wake up.

While he sat, he thought about what had triggered her anxiety, and he wanted to throttle Theo. Unfortunately, Knox knew that if Knox let Theo know he'd upset Jade, Theo would double down on his behavior. That meant ignoring him was the best strategy, even though it was the last thing he wanted to do. Still, it wasn't his call. He'd have to discuss it with Jade before doing anything.

They might not have put a label what they'd shared, but it was more than a one-night stand or *just sex*. Jade had big-time abandonment issues, thanks to her mother and her unorthodox childhood and then to the two assholes she'd agreed to marry in the past. Jade didn't realize it, but she'd already broken her man fast with Knox. And now, he'd need patience to show her he was different from those other men. *They* were different.

He turned on the television and put on ESPN. Between Holly's wedding appointments, work, trying to figure out how to get Jade in his life, and Theo causing trouble, hockey playoffs were the last thing on his mind. But no sooner had he settled in to watch television than clips of the Rockets game came on. He viewed the game for a few minutes, looking for his brother. And he found him. As Knox watched, Theo took his goalie stick and slashed an unsuspecting forward on the back of the legs.

Knox winced. He grabbed the remote and re-wound, watching the play again. Theo was such a stupid fuck. It was rare for a goalie to get suspended but no doubt that would be the end result. Especially since Cooke had to be helped off the ice. Knox shook his head, wondering how many games' suspension Theo would get this time.

JADE WOKE UP slowly, her head foggy from medication, her mouth dry. She blinked and her eyes focused on the darkened room. Sunlight streamed from behind the shades, so she knew it was still daytime. How long had she been asleep? Her head still hurt but the pounding had lessened enough that she could get up and walk around without feeling her temples throb with every step.

She glanced over and saw the other side of her bed was empty. Her stomach dipped in dismay. Knox had obviously gone home, not that she blamed him. Who wanted to sit around while she slept off her pain? It'd been sweet of him to bring her home and stick around until she fell asleep, but she couldn't deny being disappointed that he wasn't the perfect guy. The one who'd stay.

She walked into her bathroom, washed her face,

brushed her teeth, and her stomach let out a deep growl. "Lovely," she muttered, wondering what she had in the kitchen that she'd be in the mood for. Usually after a migraine, she craved carbs.

She stepped out of her bedroom and was surprised to hear a cell phone ring. Only it wasn't her ringtone but Knox's.

He'd stayed? She smiled despite herself.

"What do you want now, Celia?" Knox asked.

Celia was his ex-wife, and Jade was surprised he still spoke to her. Jade paused in the entrance to the living room, where Knox sat on the sofa, the television on a sports channel.

"No, I'm not happy to hear from you. What do you want?" he asked, annoyance in his tone.

Jade felt like an eavesdropper in her own home. She took a quiet step, hoping to walk to the kitchen without being noticed, but Knox turned and his gaze met hers.

"No, we can't have dinner. I already have plans." He gestured for Jade to come over.

She walked toward him as he continued his call.

"Who do I have dinner plans with? None of your business. We're divorced. And for the record? Whenever you call and whatever you ask me to do? Assume I'm busy." He disconnected and placed the phone on the cocktail table in front of him with a groan. "Sorry about that. Come sit. How are you feeling?"

"It's manageable now. You stayed?" She hadn't meant to blurt that out, at least not right away.

A confused expression crossed his face. "Of course I stayed. I wanted to make sure you were okay. And I ordered us dinner." He gestured to the bags on the dining room table. "I hope you're in the mood for Italian. If not, we can get something else."

Reaching out, he clasped her hand and helped her lower herself to the couch beside him.

"I… I don't know what to say. Thank you." She'd eat the Italian because he'd cared enough to think about her needs. And if she'd been craving a Belgian waffle from the diner on the corner, he didn't have to know. The Italian food sounded much better now. "Was that Celia on the phone? Your ex-wife?"

He nodded. "She showed up on my doorstep the Sunday after the gala, talking about making things right. I'm pretty sure that she's just upset that I'm moving on in a public way. Much like Theo is with you."

Jade wrinkled her nose. "I'm not sure I understand why either of them would care, considering they caused the break-ups in the first place."

"You sound like a rational human being. Theo and Celia are not. Which reminds me, there's something I wanted to tell you. You can't let Theo get to you the way he did today. He's not worth it. His opinion, his thoughts, nothing he says to you matters."

She sighed. "You're right." The call had just brought back a lot of bad memories, of feeling not good enough when she'd discovered Theo was cheating on her.

"The other thing you can't do is let him know he upset you. Once Theo is aware of what veins to slice, he'll keep on doing it."

She pressed her palms against her gritty eyes. "Why didn't I see this in him when we were together?" She glanced up and met Knox's gaze.

"Don't be so hard on yourself. He knows how to act. He let you see the needy, sad, *nobody understands me* version of Theo. He's damned good at playing that role."

"And I fell for it because I liked being needed," she muttered.

"Which is not a bad quality to have." Knox's mouth lifted in a sexy smile. "Now, before you work yourself up again, let's eat."

"Sounds good."

He insisted on setting out the plates and serving the food. He also refused to let her help him clean up. Instead, he sent her to shower or do whatever she needed to in the bedroom. He was bossy in a way she couldn't help but appreciate. And she knew that if he was sick, she'd look after him the same way.

By the time he walked into the bedroom, she'd showered and changed into lightweight leisure clothes; a pair of soft elastic waist sweats and a loose but cropped T-shirt. Her headache had eased enough that she thought it would be gone by morning, leaving her with a migraine hangover. She'd be shaky and a bit weak, but it was much better than the pain of today.

"You look comfortable," Knox said, his gaze landing on the strip of bare skin along her stomach.

"So do you." He'd ditched his sport jacket when he'd walked into the apartment and he'd rolled up his sleeves, revealing his tanned, toned forearms.

With the pain gone, she was able to focus on other things. Like how, despite their long day, he appeared every bit as sexy now as he'd been earlier today.

"Don't look at me like that," he said in a gruff voice. "You're in pain."

She shook her head. "Not anymore. Someone very special made sure I was well taken care of. And now that I feel better, I want you."

He stared at her, obviously surprised. "Are you sure you're up to it?"

She reached for the hem of her top, pulling it up and over her head, revealing her bare breasts. "Does that answer your question?"

He swallowed hard and his hand reached down to

adjust his clearly hard cock. "Works for me. I like that we're making a habit of this, because I always want you."

Her heart squeezed in her chest, and with the sensation came the realization that she was getting in deep with him. "One more night."

He stepped forward and cupped her breasts in his hands. "Whatever you say, beautiful."

Which meant, of course, that he wasn't buying her words any more than she was. But then his thumbs brushed over her nipples, and for the rest of the night, she thought only of him.

JADE'S EYES OPENED as she awakened from a drugged sleep. She was cocooned in warmth, with Knox's large body wrapped around her. She couldn't deny how much she enjoyed being with him or how much her growing feelings for him scared her. But that didn't stop her from cuddling into him.

"You're awake." His morning-roughened voice sounded deep and sexy in her ear.

"Mmm. I am."

"How are you feeling? Because if anything we did brought your headache back, I won't be happy."

"Everything we did was worth it," she assured him. Mostly because she hadn't been in terrible pain at the time.

"Good." He snuggled his chin into her shoulder. "And now?"

She blinked, testing her eyes, aware of a dull throb behind them, but nothing terrible. "It's manageable," she murmured. "It'll take some time to work its way out of my system, but all you did was make me feel better." No man had ever made her feel as good.

Out of necessity, she rolled out of his embrace. "I need the bathroom." She rose and ran into the washroom, shutting the door behind her. After taking care of business, she brushed her teeth, washed her face, and took a quick shower. After drying off, she slipped out of the bathroom and found a large T-shirt that covered her to her knees. She'd swiped it from one of her brothers when they'd been at her parents' pool.

She pulled on a pair of underwear beneath and turned to Knox. He sat up in bed, one arm behind his head, the comforter covering him to the waist.

His tanned, bare chest tempted her to join him, but he tossed the covers off. "Don't look at me like that. I need to shower, too."

She grinned. "Tell that to your…" She gestured to his thickening erection.

He laughed. "If I didn't have to get going, I would drag you into the shower along with me." He winked and strode to the bathroom. The shower water turned on soon after.

She groaned and turned, intending to make the bed, when her doorbell rang.

She walked out of her room and went to answer the door. Nobody from the front desk had called, so she assumed one of her family members or Lauren had come to see her. No one else had permission to come up.

She swung her door open and came face-to-face with her ex-fiancé. His eyes were bloodshot, his dark hair a mess, he had a bruise on his cheek, and his clothes were disheveled. The man she knew never went out looking less than perfect. Even if he'd been hurt in a game, his appearance was always model perfect.

"Theo. What are you doing here? Better yet, how did you get past the doorman?" Aware she wasn't wearing a bra, she folded her arms across her chest, protecting herself from his prying eyes.

"I waited for the old man to take a break, then slipped past him. I practically lived here. I know the routine, remember?"

"Don't remind me." She wrinkled her nose. "What do you want?"

He leaned his shoulder against the doorframe. "My life is a mess. It's been going downhill since we broke up—"

"Since I found out you were cheating," she corrected him.

He let out a groan. "It was a mistake, okay? Knox always knew how to push my buttons, and I wanted to get back at him. If you think about it, it had nothing to do with you. Not directly." He pushed past her until he was inside her apartment.

Some things never changed… especially his inability to accept responsibility or take a hint. She rubbed her palms against her burning eyes. "Get out."

"Just listen. Last night I was given a match penalty, game misconduct, and a four-game suspension."

"For doing what?" She forced herself to focus on him despite the sudden return of her headache.

He glanced down, avoiding her gaze. "High-sticked Daniel Cooke and injured him," he muttered. "I took out my frustration about you and Knox on a guy I can't stand. I couldn't concentrate on the game. But I can fix things. I just need you back. Then everything will get better. For both of us. I swear."

Her mouth opened wide as shock reverberated through her. "No, no, and no!" she said.

"In case you didn't understand her, that was a *hell no!* Not happening." Knox strode up beside her and looped an arm around her shoulders.

He was still warm from the shower, his hair was damp, he smelled good… and his chest was bare. He had one towel wrapped around his waist and another one hung over his shoulder.

She glanced at Theo and saw a vein pulsing in his temple. And his jaw was clenched tight. "What the fuck? You're here?"

Knox read the room and pulled her closer to him.

Which meant things were about to explode.

★ ★ ★

WHEN KNOX STEPPED out of the shower and opened the door to clear the mirror, he heard voices. Wrapping the towel tighter around his waist, he edged closer to the doorway to find out who was visiting. When he heard Theo's voice, he just reacted, coming to Jade's rescue, with or without clothes.

"What the fuck? You're here?"

Knox stared at his stepbrother. The guy looked like shit. Then again, it wasn't a surprise after what had gone down on the ice last night.

Feeling protective, Knox drew Jade closer.

"Let's back up. Did you just say it's *our* fault you high-sticked Daniel Cooke into the boards and now have to sit out a four-game suspension during the playoffs?"

"You always have to fuck up my life. Why Jade?" he asked like a sulky child.

"Why Celia?" Knox replied. They'd never had a

conversation about what had gone down between them. Not since Theo's betrayal. If this was going to be it, Knox might as well say what was on his mind. "You were engaged to Jade. You'd recently been traded to New York. You had everything going for you. So what did you do? You slept with my wife, asshole. So maybe you should ask yourself, who fucked up whose life?"

Jade stiffened and pulled herself away. "This sounds like something you two need to figure out."

Shit. He thought back to what he'd said and realized she might have misinterpreted his reaction. She headed toward the bedroom when Theo reached out and grabbed her arm.

She attempted to jerk free but Theo held tight.

"Let her go," Knox said, barely maintaining control.

"I just want to talk——"

Knox cut Theo off with a fist to his jaw, sending him stumbling. "You don't grab a woman. Especially not one who doesn't want anything to do with you."

Knox braced for a return blow but it never came.

Jade stared, not at Knox with any kind of horror but at Theo, a scowl on her face. "Theo, go home. Take some time and figure out your life. But leave me out of it."

She spun around and walked back to the bedroom,

apparently leaving Knox to take out the trash. In the end, Theo left of his own accord, the look on his face promising retribution.

After locking up, Knox fixed his towel and returned to the bedroom. Jade was pacing.

"Are you okay?" he asked.

"What the fuck was that?" she asked, sounding pissed.

He raised an eyebrow. "The punch? He had it coming. Don't expect me to let him manhandle you without reacting."

She blew out a breath. "No. I have four brothers. I knew what was going to happen. I just thought he'd come back at you."

"When he's on the ice, adrenaline keeps him going. But off it? I doubt he's got the balls to hit me back."

Jade nodded. "Actually, I was talking about him showing up here." She sat down on the edge of the bed. "I don't understand. Why does he suddenly want me back?"

"He's unraveling. Nothing's going his way and the fact that we're together is a trigger for him."

"Should I worry about him?" she asked, shaken that he'd slipped past the doorman.

"He always calms down." Knox moved closer and placed his hand beneath her chin, tipping her head to meet his gaze. "But his reaction is not our problem."

"Is him blowing up your marriage a problem?" she asked, looking him in the eyes.

"My marriage was over long before Celia slept with Theo. But if she hadn't cheated, I probably would have stayed with her and tried to make it work." He hated admitting that. It made him feel weak.

"Why?" Jade placed her hand on his.

"Because I saw how it killed my father when my mother left. I promised myself I'd never walk out when things got tough. That I'd try to make things work." He dipped his head. "But I drew the line at cheating."

"So you aren't still in love with her."

He shook his head. "No. That was a wrong choice of words earlier. Theo didn't fuck up my life. But he did fuck up yours. As a brother, though, he betrayed me."

"God, why won't he leave me alone? I'm over him, but dealing with his drama is exhausting."

They sat in silence, Knox trying to decide where things stood between them now.

"Are you working today?" he finally asked.

"No. I'm still not feeling great from the migraine meds. I could use a day off. I'll call Lauren. I just need to go back to bed and rest."

Knox took that as his cue. "I'll get dressed and head out, then," he said.

And Jade didn't ask him to stay.

Chapter Seven

JADE HAD HAD a hellishly long week, and she'd worked all weekend, so she was more tired than usual. She attributed it to the migraine she'd had this past Tuesday and the hangover from the headache and meds that had followed. She'd canceled girls' night with Lauren and slept through dinner and woke up early Sunday morning. But she still felt off.

On top of being wiped out, she still felt sick about that scene with Theo. She hadn't heard from him since, and though she was relieved, she was also on edge. She hadn't seen this unstable side of him before, and she didn't like it. And she really didn't like the fact that, for some reason, he'd decided to focus on her once more.

Knox had left for his guys' trip to Vegas and she missed him. She couldn't stop thinking about how he'd taken care of her when she'd had her migraine. As an adult, she wasn't used to having someone around when she was sick. It felt good to know he'd wanted to stay with her. He'd checked on her prior to leaving but she hadn't heard from him since he'd left for his trip.

And that was fine. That was the way she wanted things between them. Casual. Occasional one-night stands worked for her. They weren't a couple and he didn't owe her anything. If she'd come to rely on hearing from him at bedtime, this break was a good reminder that nothing was permanent.

After Jade finished drying her hair, her cell rang and Aurora's name flashed on the screen.

Smiling, Jade answered. "Hey!"

"Hi! So, do you want to go shopping with me? We can meet up with Nick for lunch when we're finished," her sister-in-law said.

"Where is Leah?" Jade wondered if the little spitfire would join them.

Aurora laughed. "I pawned her off on Melly," she said of her pseudo-mother, the woman who'd taken her in when her oldest brother found her after their father died. She was his father's illegitimate daughter— the one he'd hidden away, the one who'd grown up in foster care. Linc Kingston had brought Aurora home to his mother's house, eighteen and pregnant. Aurora and Melly had bonded, and now, Aurora considered Melly to be Leah's grandmother.

"You know what? I'd love to get out of this apartment. Where do you want to go?"

"The Americana okay with you?" Aurora asked,

mentioning the outdoor mall in Manhasset, near where she and Nick lived on Long Island.

"Perfect." Some fresh air would be good for her.

They agreed on a time, and after getting ready, Jade took an Uber and met her sister-in-law outside Gucci.

On a normal day, Jade wasn't one to splurge on big-ticket items, but she was feeling off and thought that spoiling herself might make her feel better. She bought a Gucci everyday tote and a necklace with a *J* amulet on a thick chain at David Yurman.

She tried on and purchased casual clothes because she really wanted to have more time to herself. She considered the items an incentive, to persuade her to hang out at home more often and delegate more. Hell, maybe she'd even hire another planner. Give herself some breathing room.

"And then I found your brother in our bed with a stripper."

Jade sighed.

Aurora nudged her arm and they paused by one of the stores. "You haven't heard a word I've said." She stepped up beside Jade, juggling packages of her own. "Are you okay?"

She nodded. "Sorry. I'm a little out of it today."

"It's okay." Aurora studied her with concern. "Let's eat. That always gives me a second wind." Aurora glanced at her phone. "Nick's here. Where do you want to have lunch? We can ask him to meet us there."

"There are only two restaurants in the mall unless he wants to drive us all somewhere else," Jade said.

"How about the modern Asian restaurant? I've been dying to try it. They have sushi and salads with seafood."

Her stomach churned at the thought, and she pressed her hands against her belly. "God no. No seafood. I'm not in the mood today." If she even looked at that menu, she thought she'd be sick. "How about a diner? I'd rather eat something bland."

"Sure." Aurora glanced at her cell. "I'll tell Nick to pick us up here, and we'll go to the one up the street."

Jade smiled. "Thanks. I promise next time we can go anywhere you want. I've just been feeling off since that migraine."

Aurora squeezed her hand. "No worries." She texted Nick, and after meeting up with him, they all went for lunch.

★   ★   ★

KNOX SAT IN the dark of the gentleman's club he and his friends frequented when in Vegas. Neon lights provided a multi-sensory environment that he knew would cause Jade to suffer with one of her migraines. And that was the problem he'd been having this entire trip.

Instead of enjoying drinking with the guys, he was worrying about how Jade was feeling. When he ate at the best restaurants, he thought about how much Jade would enjoy the meal. Instead of taking in the ambience, he was thinking about how it would impact Jade. And wouldn't Asher be pissed to know that? Neither of them had brought up his relationship with Jade this weekend, and that was for the best.

The guys around him were drunk, and though Knox had had his share of alcohol, he could barely feel it. In fact, he wanted nothing more than to go back to his room, even though the show hadn't even started yet.

"How can a guy look so preoccupied when he's surrounded by gorgeous women serving him drinks, with the option for a lap dance coming up any minute?" Derek Bettencourt, son of Senator and presidential candidate Corbin Bettencourt and Knox's close friend, slid into the empty seat beside him.

"I don't know what you're talking about." Knox raised his glass and took a sip before gesturing to the server for another.

"Make it two," Derek said.

The gorgeous brunette leaned close to Knox, her breasts brushing his arm, and picked up his empty glass. "Sure thing," she said in a husky voice, meeting his gaze.

"Thank you."

She strode off in her ultra-high heels and with an added sway of her hips.

"She's interested," Derek said. "You should go for it."

Knox had no doubt he could charm her up to his room if he wanted to. The problem was, he didn't want to, so he ignored the suggestion.

"Is your father still trying to convince you to join him when he announces his intention to run?" he asked Derek.

"Of course he is. Presenting himself as a family man is very important to him. But I have no intention of indulging his fantasy. He's done just fine without me by his side since I turned eighteen and could decide for myself what I would and wouldn't do."

Knox laughed. "It must drive him crazy not to be able to control you."

Derek nodded. "Can't say my sister's being any more malleable lately."

Derek's younger sister was a model with a difficult reputation, but Knox knew she and Derek were close.

"Your parents ended up with headstrong children," Knox agreed.

"Or our nannies did," Derek muttered.

"Here you go, gentleman." Their server leaned

down, giving Knox a full view of her ample cleavage. She placed both drinks on the table and slipped a piece of paper into the breast pocket of Knox's sport jacket, patting it with her hand.

Then she sashayed away, walking to the next table.

"See?" Derek raised an eyebrow. "Are you going to tap that?"

Smirking, Knox pulled out the paper and slid it into Derek's breast pocket with a double pat.

"Okay, time's up. Who's got you tied up in knots?" Derek asked.

Knox lifted his fresh bourbon and took a long sip. "I don't know what you're talking about."

"You haven't been yourself since you got here. You're usually the outgoing, wild one, and you always pick up women when you're here. And that one was hot." He gestured to the woman carrying drinks to another table.

Knox blew out a deep breath. Derek was his closest friend and had been since business school. He knew Derek wouldn't repeat anything Knox said to him, not even to Asher. Derek and Asher were friends, but they weren't as tight as Knox and Derek were.

"There's someone," Knox admitted.

"Someone special."

Knox ran a hand over the back of his neck. "Yeah. But it's complicated."

Derek leaned forward, his head close. "Who?"

"Asher's sister." It felt good to get the truth off his chest.

"Aah, shit." Derek shook his head. "When you do it up, you do it up right." He lifted his bourbon in a toast.

Knox touched his glass to his. "Amen."

"Does he know?" He tipped his head toward Jade's brother, who was talking to the brunette who'd hit on Knox. Apparently, she wasn't fussy about which man she went upstairs with, as long as she got lucky.

"He knows about the first couple of times," Knox muttered.

Derek slapped the table, threw his head back, and laughed. "Considering what you're giving up here and the beating you might have to take from Asher, I'm betting she's worth it."

"She is." But the joke might be on him. Jade had so many hang-ups when it came to relationships, the way Knox felt, not to mention what he was willing to go through or give up, might not matter.

But he was willing to try.

Right now, he was giving her what she seemed to need. Space. After that scene with Theo, Jade had been quiet and withdrawn. She'd accepted his explanation about his marriage and seemed to believe him, but when he'd gone to kiss her goodbye, he'd felt her resistance. He blamed Theo. Before that visit, they'd been growing closer.

But he was learning about what made Jade tick. She'd pulled back, and he'd taken the hint. He knew insinuating himself into her daily life wouldn't do him any good right now. Other than checking on her after her migraine, he'd decided to back off and give her a chance to miss him.

That was the reason he'd decided to go through with this guys' weekend. But he hated every second of not hearing her voice. He consoled himself with the fact that Jade and Holly had a florist appointment early next week and Knox planned to be there.

With any luck, she'd have missed him as much as he missed her. And then, just maybe, she might be more open to the idea of a relationship.

JADE WOKE UP the morning of her floral appointment with Holly and barely made it to the bathroom before she threw up. God. A stomach virus was the last thing she needed. Though she attempted to shower and go to work, coffee didn't stay in her stomach, and she ended up back in bed.

She dialed Lauren.

"Good morning, sunshine," Lauren said.

Jade managed a smile. "Not such a good one. I'm

not feeling well. Think you can handle the floral appointment with Holly today?"

"Of course. What's wrong?"

Her stomach twisted uncomfortably and she moaned. "I'm nauseous. I think I've picked up a stomach bug."

"You've been exhausted for over a week. Take today and tomorrow off. This weekend's event schedule is light. You don't need to be hands-on for every party. The girls and I can handle it. I'm ordering you to rest," Lauren said.

Jade managed a laugh. "So, you're the boss now?"

"No. I'm the boss's best friend. So please listen to me? I've been worried about you. Even a bad migraine never hits quite this bad, and for so long afterwards." Lauren's voice was filled with concern.

Jade blew out a long breath. "Okay. I'll take a few days off."

"Good. Now, as your best friend, I need to ask you something, and you aren't going to like the question."

She lay on her side and stared at the photographs on her dresser. There were a few of her family and one of Jade and Lauren at the beach. The people who mattered most to her.

"Go on," Jade said warily.

"How long ago was the first time you were with

Knox? The night of the fundraiser?"

"Umm…"

"Three weeks," Lauren said, answering for her. "And have you gotten your period since then?"

Jade groaned. "Shut up. I can't be pregnant."

"Did you get your period? Because I'm pretty sure we're synced up, and I didn't see you running to the ladies' room with your purse last week. You've been exhausted, dizzy, and now you're throwing up…"

She squeezed her eyes shut tight. "Don't do this to me. I can't be pregnant," she said. But apparently, she might very well be. "Hold on."

She took her phone away from her ear, opened the browser, and did a search. Then she returned to her phone call. "Condoms are ninety-eight percent effective. Google said that means two in every one hundred women who've used them as birth control will become pregnant. The odds are in my favor," she said to Lauren.

"Who are you trying to convince? Yourself? Or me? Listen. Stay calm. How about I cancel today's appointments, stop at a drugstore, pick up a test, and then come over? You don't have to do this alone."

Jade pulled in a deep breath, which did nothing to calm the rapid, panicked beat of her heart. "No. You have to meet with Holly. But promise me you will not say a word to Knox. Nothing more than I wasn't feeling well. Got it?"

"Got it. You know you can trust me," Lauren promised.

"I do and thank you." Lauren was like a sister to her. She'd protect her secrets.

"Now, you swear you'll let me know if there is any news to share?"

"I promise." And with a little luck, there would be no real secrets to hide. Just a false alarm.

She never thought there'd come a day when she wished for a stomach virus. But today was that day.

AS MUCH AS Knox loved his sister, he couldn't give two shits about which flowers she picked for her wedding. Once again, he wished her mother was here to help her, but given the situation, there was nothing he could do but grit his teeth and deal with it. Her fiancé couldn't make it today, so Knox had to step up his game. The upside was that he'd finally see Jade again. He was hoping to have some alone time with her, to tell her how much he'd missed her.

When he and Holly walked into the florist, they were immediately surrounded by multicolored blooms and fragrant scents. He looked around for Jade and was surprised when Lauren walked out of the back room with a woman who was untying a heavy and well-pocketed apron from around her neck. She said something to Lauren, then walked behind the main counter, while Lauren headed their way.

"Holly! Knox! It's so good to see you both," Lauren said, smiling at them.

"You, too! Is Jade coming?" Holly asked before Knox could phrase the question more delicately. His sister was as enamored of Jade as he was.

Lauren glanced from him to Holly. "She's not feeling well and sends her regrets. But I promise you're in good hands with me. And I'll run everything by Jade later on."

"What's wrong?" Knox asked, concerned. Last week she'd had a migraine and now she was missing what he knew she'd consider an important appointment. That wasn't like her. Even if she wanted to avoid him, he knew she wouldn't disappoint his sister on purpose.

"Stomach bug," Lauren said, then turned toward the counter. "Devon, are you ready?" she asked.

Knox ground his teeth in frustration. What was going on? Just then, Devon walked over and introduced herself, and he had no choice but to sit down and talk about flowers.

Knox sat beside Holly but pulled out his cell and sent Jade a text message asking if she was okay and if he could bring her anything after the appointment.

Because one way or another, Jade's apartment was his next stop.

For the next two hours, they looked at photographs and discussed flower colors and varieties for the wedding day. Devon asked Holly if she wanted a bridal arch, which led to a thirty-minute discussion of the pros and cons of having one. All the while, Knox kept an eye on his phone, but Jade didn't reply.

He'd already decided giving her space hadn't been the right approach, but he'd been too busy at work to see her in person, and he couldn't say what he wanted on a phone call. He'd been counting on seeing her today, but her silence had him on edge.

Maybe she was sleeping. The thought didn't ease the twisting in his gut that told him that she was avoiding him. And her reasons had nothing to do with her being sick.

PREGNANT. JADE STARED at the three sticks, all different brands she'd purchased, just to be sure. She wasn't stupid enough to wonder how it had happened. She was just damned unlucky when she looked at the odds.

Her cell beeped. With her stomach churning and not just from nausea, she glanced at the screen. Lauren had texted her:

Appointment over. Knox said he was going to check on you.

Thank God for good friends, Jade thought, replying with a heart emoji.

There was no way she was up to a conversation with the man who'd fathered the baby she was carrying. Not when she'd yet to come to terms with it herself. Besides, she hadn't heard from him when he was away and though she thought she'd missed him, she now chalked it up to pregnancy hormones and being overly emotional.

So she pulled out her carry-on and threw some clothing and other necessities into the suitcase. Although she'd rather just disappear, she had to stop and talk to her oldest brother first. She pulled up her ride share app and called for a car.

Not long after, she found herself sitting across from Asher in his new office. One of the best things about her family was that they'd drop everything for each other, no matter what.

Asher rose and sat on the edge of the mahogany desk, his concerned gaze on hers. He reached out and placed a hand on her knee. "Stop the nervous tapping and talk to me."

She swallowed hard. "I need to get away. Can I take the plane to your house on Windermere?" Asher owned an estate on the island off Eleuthera, near the

Bahamas. There was no better place for her to be alone and think.

"You can go anytime you want, but I need to ask, what's wrong?"

She breathed in and out, controlling her rolling belly. "Can it wait? I'm not ready to talk about it yet."

He studied her. "Are you okay? Do you want me or someone else to come with you?"

She shook her head. "I just need time to think where no one can find me."

He opened his mouth as if to ask another question, then closed it again. He paused for long seconds. "I'll tell my pilot to fuel the plane, and he'll be waiting when you get there."

She jumped up from her seat and hugged her big brother. "Thank you. And thanks for not pushing me for information. I promise to talk when I'm ready."

He set her back and kissed her cheek. "I do have conditions."

"What might those be?" she asked warily.

"Check in daily. I need to know you're all right, and the only way I can do that is if I hear your voice."

Her heart squeezed in her chest. "Because you're worried I might be like Mom?"

"No. Of course not. Why would you say that?"

She would always remember the conversation she'd overheard her brothers having when Jade was eight. They believed that, because she was a daughter, Jade was more likely to have inherited Audrey's mental illness. When she'd grown up and had gone through therapy of her own, she'd discovered the flaw in their thinking. But it had been too many years of internalizing their words and being afraid of every mood swing she had. Her anxiety attacks had begun after hearing that conversation, and she'd worked hard to fight them ever since.

"Jade?" Asher's voice snapped her back to the present.

"I don't know. It was a stupid thing to say."

Asher studied her warily, his eyes narrowed. He was smart but he couldn't read her mind. The men in her family had no idea what she'd overheard, and she never planned to tell them. Her siblings would be devastated to know their words had hurt her. Not even Serenity was aware of the words that still haunted her.

"Don't worry. I'll check in," she promised.

He let out a groan. "Okay. I see you have your bag with you. Take my driver to the airport."

She knew better than to argue with him. "Thanks. Will you let Mom and Dad know I'm fine? Tell them I just took a little vacation, okay?"

"Sure. If you decide you want to talk, I'll be there, okay?"

She nodded. "You're a good brother." She squeezed his hand in thanks.

He picked up his phone and called his driver. And before she knew it, Jade was on her way out of the country for some serious self-reflection and a whole lot of panic.

AFTER THE MEETING with the florist, Knox took a taxi to Jade's apartment, only for the doorman to tell him she wasn't home. The information was contrary to what Lauren had said, and he got back in his car, frustrated. She didn't return any of his texts or calls and his worry grew.

On Wednesday, he arrived at Jade's office by ten a.m., only to be greeted with the news that she wasn't in the office today. Unwilling to give up, he asked to see Lauren instead, hoping she'd open up to him. Because he was damned sure something was wrong.

When Lauren stepped out of her office, she didn't appear surprised to see him. "Come on in, Knox." She gestured for him to follow her into her office.

He waited until she closed the door behind him and turned to face her. "Where is she?"

"I told you she's not feeling well." She walked around him and sat down behind her desk.

"Then why isn't she home?" A panicked thought

hit him. "She's not in the hospital, is she?"

Lauren shook her head. "No, nothing like that."

He ground his teeth together. "Then what is it like, Lauren?" He braced his hands on her desk and leaned over until he was edging into her personal space.

"Believe me, if I could tell you, I would. But best friends protect each other. Just give her some time."

He lowered his head and groaned. He didn't want to respect Lauren or her loyalty, but he did, and he was glad Jade had a best friend she could trust. He just wished it wasn't at his expense.

He drew up straighter. "Fine. Give me something. Please."

Lauren rolled a pencil between her palms, obviously thinking. "I can't tell you anything, but there's someone else you can ask. If you can get past him, then I figure you deserve to find her."

"Cryptic," he muttered.

"But not difficult." She raised her eyebrows and smiled for the first time. "Good luck, Knox. You're going to need it."

He wondered if she was referring to him having to deal with Asher? Or Jade.

He met Lauren's gaze. "Thank you."

She treated him to a brief smile. "I hope you're as good a guy as I think you are. Jade deserves that in a man."

He inclined his head and walked out, heading to the elevator. When he stepped onto the street, he pulled out his phone and called Asher's work number. Knox wouldn't bother his friend on his cell in case he was tied up... which ended up being the case.

According to Asher's secretary, he would be in meetings all day. With no other leads or people to ask, Knox hailed a taxi and asked to be taken to the Warriors' stadium. Keeping focused wasn't easy and the day dragged on. In the car on his way home, he dialed Asher's cell, but the call went straight to voicemail, and Knox resigned himself to having to wait until tomorrow.

He ordered in dinner and had a shitty night's sleep. First thing the next morning, he called Asher's cell and asked if they could meet. This wasn't a conversation Knox wanted to have over the phone. Asher said to meet him at the new office space he'd described in proud detail while they were in Vegas.

Knox took a ride share to Midtown West where the renamed Dirty Dare Spirits offices was located. The interior architectural design was impressive. Four bars were spread out on the ground level, serving a variety of coffee and alcohol, depending on the time of day. And a separate floor held a lab where mixologists created craft cocktails. Asher's description hadn't done the place justice.

Once inside, Knox checked in with the security guard and handed the man his identification. The guard called upstairs, confirmed his appointment, and returned the license before directing Knox to the bank of elevators.

A few minutes later, he met up with a receptionist, who led him past the glass-enclosed offices and stopped at the door at the end of the hall.

She knocked, and when Asher's voice instructed her to come in, she turned the knob and motioned for Knox to step past her.

"Thanks, Grace. Shut the door, please." Asher rose from his desk and walked around to greet Knox.

They shook hands and Asher gestured for him to sit. "Can I get you coffee?"

He shook his head. "No, thanks."

Asher lowered himself into the chair beside him. "What brings you by? It sounded urgent."

"I'm worried about your sister." Knox decided to jump in with the truth.

"No need to be. She's fine." Asher picked a nonexistent piece of lint off his suit jacket.

Knox groaned. "Are we really going to play games? We're old friends. You know you can trust me."

Asher held up his hands in defeat. "All I know is that she told me she needed time to think, and I promised to respect that as long as she checked in with me every day."

"When did she leave?" Knox asked.

"Two days ago."

Damn. He wondered if Lauren had tipped her off to the fact that he'd planned to stop by.

"And you heard from her today?"

Asher nodded. "If I thought something was very wrong, I'd have gone with her."

"Where?" Knox gripped the handles on his chair. "Where is Jade?"

"Why do you want to know? Because she's my sister and I don't want to betray her confidence." Leaning back in his seat, Asher crossed one leg over the other.

Knox pinched the bridge of his nose, feeling a building headache coming on. "I don't appreciate having to tell you anything before I talk to Jade, but if it's the only way you'll divulge her location, fine."

Asher remained silent. Waiting.

Knox shook his head. "One day you're going to fall in love, and I hope it bites you in the ass," he muttered. "Then you can think back to today and regret the smug way you're forcing me to pull information out of you, piece by piece."

Asher sat up straighter and coughed. "You're in love with my sister?"

"Not that I planned to share it with you, but yes, I

am. And I'm worried about her. She was supposed to be at the florist meeting with my sister two days ago and she didn't show up. Lauren said she had a stomach virus, but when I went to her apartment to check on her, the doorman told me she wasn't home. She must have been with you."

Asher lowered his shoulders and groaned. "I had no idea you two had gotten serious."

"If it makes you feel any better, I don't think Jade realizes it yet, either."

He let out a loud laugh. "Jesus. She's keeping you at arm's length, isn't she?"

"She sure as hell is. But something caused her to run, and I need to find out what it is. So?" The ball was in Asher's court. He'd either help Knox or turn him away.

"She's at my house on Windermere. She showed up here with a carry-on bag and asked if she could go there for a few days. She took the jet."

At least she'd gone somewhere familiar and safe. "She didn't say why she needed to leave?"

"She didn't." Asher braced his hands on the chair and stood. "But I take it you want to head down there and find out."

It wasn't a question and Knox didn't think it warranted an answer. Yes, Knox had work to do. Yes, he had an upcoming season to focus on. But he trusted his coaches and managers to handle anything leading up to pre-season training camp. But even if his team was heading into the Super Bowl, Jade would still be his priority.

He rose to his feet.

"The jet's back at Teterboro airport. I'll have my pilot fuel up and get ready to go. You two are giving him a workout," Asher said as he walked around his desk and picked up his phone.

When he was finished issuing orders, Asher leveled Knox with what Knox had come to think of as his big-brother glare. "Don't make me regret this."

"That's not my intention." He started for the door and turned. "Asher, thanks."

His friend inclined his head. "And good luck to you," Asher said.

Knox knew he was going to need it.

Chapter Eight

J ADE HAD ARRIVED at the island and slept for almost two days. Maggie, the housekeeper, took care of her, bringing Jade's meals to her room. Jade knew Maggie well since she'd worked for Serenity and Michael from the time Jade was thirteen and Layla was born, until Serenity no longer needed her. Asher had then hired her to run the island estate.

Her second day here, Jade felt somewhat better. She showered and came out for dinner. Her brother also had a live-in chef for himself and guests who came to visit, and he'd called ahead for her arrival. She ate a delicious chicken, rice, and broccoli dinner, relieved she could keep the food down. After, she made her way to her room, watched some television and turned in for the night.

Exhaustion had become her new best friend, and it felt so good to know she could crash and not worry about work the next day. She slept late and ate the healthiest breakfast she'd had in a long time, sitting outside on a veranda overlooking the ocean. She tipped her head and took in the blue sky. The sun shone overhead with a few white fluffy clouds. If not for the slight queasiness in her stomach reminding her why she'd had to escape to paradise, things would be perfect.

She placed her hand over her still-flat belly and sighed. It wasn't like she was here to decide what to do. As soon as the plane had taken off—and she'd left New York and the pressure behind—she'd known what she wanted. She would have this baby. But she needed to decide how to approach Knox about it. On top of not knowing how he'd react, she also worried about what her child might inherit from her. Migraines? Worse?

"Thank you, biological mom," she muttered.

Jade was sure most of her issues came from the parent she'd never known. Anxiety accompanied her most days, and in the back of her mind, she lived in fear of ending up like her mother. Even though she'd become pregnant without having thought it through, she reassured herself that she could be the mother Audrey Dare had never been. Still, the possibilities frightened her.

After breakfast, she called Asher as promised, assuring him she was okay but not sharing her news. Knox needed to hear it before anyone else, and he would... as soon as she managed to get a handle on her fears. Next, she FaceTimed with Lauren, assuring her friend she was fine, she just needed time.

"Knox is losing his mind," Lauren told her. "He came by the office today and he wasn't happy when I wouldn't give him any information."

Jade let out a sigh. "You're the best friend a girl could have. I'm not trying to torture him. I just want to come to terms with all the changes I'm going to be dealing with before I bring him into it. And besides, I haven't heard from him since his return from Vegas. Why is he suddenly looking for me?"

Her friend tucked her sleek bob behind one ear. "I don't know, but his expression when you weren't at Holly's appointment was pure disappointment."

Jade bit down on her lower lip. "I'll text him and let him know there's nothing to worry about."

Lauren nodded. "I think that's the right thing to do."

"Agreed. So how's work?"

Lauren rolled her eyes. "You took time off. Use it. Everything here is under control. Even Holly," she said, laughing.

"Okay. I'll talk to you tomorrow." Jade blew her friend a kiss and Lauren did the same before they cut off the video call.

Before she could change her mind, she texted Knox with a brief reassurance that she was okay and would be in touch. Then she shut off her phone.

Gathering her beach bag, she walked from the veranda, down the stairs, to the umbrella and chair that had been set up for her by Corey, Maggie's son, who'd moved here to be close to his mother. Asher had given him a job. He was in charge of the pool, the beach, the grounds keepers, etc. Not once had Jade ever taken her family or her financial circumstances for granted, and she whispered a thank you as she took in the beauty around her.

No sooner had she relaxed onto the cushioned recliner in the shade of the umbrella than she fell asleep. She spent most of the morning and midafternoon alternating between dozing, reading, and staring out at the ocean, hoping for a sign to guide her—something that would help her manage the unease churning inside her. Once she returned to New York and told Knox, they'd have to figure out his role in their baby's life. And she'd have to make an appointment to see an obstetrician.

But the first thing she'd have to do was talk to her psychiatrist, in actuality, a psychopharmacologist who handled her medication, to find out which medications she should discontinue and what she could do to make sure she kept the life growing inside her healthy. She'd already left him a message but hadn't heard back yet. Equally important, she needed to keep herself safe. Her mother's ultimate act was never far from her mind. More reasons for Jade to be concerned.

In this beautiful place, where she shouldn't have a care in the world, her worries were starting to overwhelm her. Needing to move, she rose from her lounger and walked along the beach, allowing the ocean waves to occasionally wash over her bare feet, then recede again. Her hair blew around her, sticking to her face and annoying her. She turned to face the house so the breeze pushed her hair off her face, helping her as she grabbed the long strands and wound them with a tie she kept on her wrist.

She blew out a breath as she took in the sprawling mansion, a white stucco manor with its long veranda… and saw a dark-haired man walking her way. She stiffened and tried to convince herself Asher had arrived to check on her, but the closer the lone figure came, the more certain she was that her visitor wasn't her brother.

"Knox." His name flew away on the heavy breeze, as she stood, nerves churning, and waited for him to reach her.

He strode closer. A pair of jeans was rolled at his ankles, his feet were bare, and a casual navy Warriors T-shirt clung to his muscular form.

He reached her, stepping into her personal space, his eyes hidden by aviators that only added to his appeal. "I have to ask. Are you running from anyone in particular? Or just me?" The sexy twist to his lips was her only indication he wasn't furious with her.

"I texted you," she said, her excuse lame and she knew it.

"A couple of hours ago. I was already in the air." He studied her behind those dark lenses. "By then, I wanted my arrival to be a surprise."

"Why are you here?" she asked.

A long strand of hair escaped her ponytail, and he reached out, tucking it behind her ear. "Because you're here."

A soft tremor rippled through her, and her nipples puckered against the small triangles of her bikini—something she'd worn because she'd thought she was alone.

She ran her tongue over her bottom lip, tasting the salt from the ocean. "How did you find me?"

He reached out and grasped her palm in his larger one. "Come on. Let's walk."

She curled her fingers around his hand and let him lead the way. He turned and they strode back toward her lounge chair, keeping their feet close enough to feel the waves pool around them.

To her surprise, he didn't ask questions. They reached her chair, to find Corey had already brought out a lounge for Knox. It was warm and she didn't think he could stay outside much longer in his jeans, but they remained for another hour. He asked her what she was reading, and they talked about the romances she surprisingly enjoyed. Despite no longer believing in happily-ever-afters for herself, she loved reading about them for the heroines of books.

"What do you like to read?" she asked him.

"Nonfiction. Anything from sports biographies, which I know makes sense, given I own a team, to Mafia history." He shrugged.

She found his interests fascinating. She found *him* fascinating. He'd flown down here to see her, but he wasn't pushing her for answers as to why she'd left. She'd tell him soon.

She looked over to where he rested in the chair beside her, sweat beading on his forehead. "Let's go inside. We can shower and you can have a drink before dinner."

If he caught on to her wording, *you can have a drink,* he didn't say.

She packed up her sunscreen and earbuds and other things, putting them in her beach bag, then strode back to the house. They walked up the steps, onto the veranda, and he opened the door for them to step inside. "Did Maggie give you a room?" she asked of the woman who ran the estate.

"She did."

Was that a smile hovering around those sexy lips?

She shrugged and they headed up the stairs to the second floor, where all the bedrooms except the master were located. "We can meet up after we shower," she said when she reached the top of the landing.

He remained silent, so she strode down the hall to her room, stopping at the closed door. She felt his heat behind her and glanced over her shoulder. "What are you doing? Which room is yours?"

He reached around her, turned the handle, and opened her door. "Right here." He pushed open the door, and she saw his suitcase sitting on the open folding luggage rack.

Her stomach fluttered and she spun around. "What did you do?"

"I told Maggie we're staying together." He stepped past her and walked to his unzipped suitcase.

And now Jade knew why he'd been so easy on her down by the beach. The man obviously had a plan, and that included making sure she couldn't escape from him again.

KNOX WAS A man who was known for his patience. As a team owner, he recognized talent and knew the virtue of allowing time to cultivate a player until his abilities shone through. True, sometimes he had to cut his losses, but he and the head coach had the same philosophy. And he was using that philosophy with Jade right now.

On the flight down, he'd debated on how to handle her when they finally came face-to-face. One part of him wanted to toss her over his shoulder, carry her back to the room, and fuck her fear out of her. But the more rational man inside him knew that approach would never work. Jade needed time and understanding.

But that didn't mean he intended to let her out of his sight again.

Her gaze moved from his suitcase to his face, her mouth opening and closing as she struggled for words. "I don't think this is a good idea."

"I disagree. Now do you want to shower first, or should I?" He waited for her to react.

If she really didn't want him here, she could storm out and demand Maggie remove his things or she could take another room for herself. He might be pushing, but the choice was still all hers.

She let out an adorable little growl, walked past him, and pulled clothing out of her drawers before storming off to the bathroom. He'd already memorized the peak of her nipples in the thin red fabric of the bikini. Now she treated him to her lush ass in the sexy bottoms before the door slammed behind her.

He grinned. One game down. But it wasn't the playoffs and it wasn't the Super Bowl. He had more work to do before he took home the overall prize. And though he didn't consider Jade a trophy to be won, he was a competitor at heart. And it was her heart he wanted to win.

He did a quick job of unpacking, then stretched out on the bed while she no doubt stewed and took her time in the bathroom. He heard the sound of the blow dryer, and more time passed before she walked out in a flirty short floral skirt and a tight tank top. Without speaking to him, she strode out and headed downstairs.

He knew her well enough to know she wasn't going to leave him on the island, and they would have their much-needed conversation. He rose, grabbed his change of clothing, showered, then made his way downstairs as well.

Maggie met him at the foot of the stairs and asked what he'd like to drink. Wanting something light, he asked for a beer. She nodded and led him toward a room that was probably the library. Books lined floor-to-ceiling shelves, and a rolling wooden ladder leaned against one wall.

Jade, her long blond hair falling in waves down her back, stood staring out a window at the lush greenery beyond. His heart beat heavier in his chest. For all his lightness earlier, he understood what was at stake.

He cleared his throat and Jade turned. "Hi," he said.

"Hi." She stepped closer. "Did you see Maggie? Did she offer you a drink or can I get you one?"

Obviously, she'd calmed down. "She's bringing me a beer. Thanks." He glanced at her empty hand and noticed there was no glass for her in the room. "You didn't want anything?"

She shook her head. "My stomach hasn't been great."

He narrowed his gaze. "You still have that same stomach virus?" He hadn't been sure Lauren was telling him the truth.

"I'm not sick." Her wary gaze met his and she folded her arms across her chest. "I'm pregnant."

The blood rushed through Knox's ears, making him doubt he'd heard Jade correctly. "You're what?"

"I'm pregnant. Do you need me to spell it out? Explain what it means?" Jade visibly curled in on herself, shoulders hunched and her fear tangible.

Though Knox knew he had to say something, shock rendered him mute. He'd been married and thought he'd have kids with Celia, but their relationship had imploded long before she'd slept with Theo. After his divorce, he believed his time for marriage and children had passed. Not that thirty-three was old but he'd been feeling jaded. Which was ironic because that sense had faded upon meeting... Jade.

"Silence. Okay, got it." She brushed past him, and only his reflexes had him nabbing her arm and stopping her.

"Wait."

She stilled.

"Give me a minute to process it, okay?" He waited for her to answer.

"Okay," she whispered.

He released her arm, and she walked over to the sofa and settled herself in the corner.

Jade was pregnant. He was going to be a father. And she'd obviously freaked the fuck out and escaped to her brother's island. The last thing she needed was Knox panicking, too.

He strode over and sat down beside her, close enough for his thigh to touch hers and to block her in. Nobody was running from this conversation.

"It's going to be okay." He placed his hand on her thigh.

She looked up at him with those dark blue eyes. "Is it? You don't seem thrilled, and that's before you learn more about me."

He already knew she had anxiety and migraines. He was aware of her mother's mental health issues, and he was certain they scared her. But he was missing a link. "I didn't say I wasn't happy. I'm in shock. Why don't you talk to me and let me in? We have to start somewhere."

She nodded and grasped his hands. "I don't know where to begin."

Then he'd start for her. "You're pregnant and it's not what you planned. How do you feel?" he asked.

"Other than nauseous?"

Her lips lifted in a smile, but he wasn't letting her get away with dodging him, and he pulled one hand free and tapped her nose. "How do you feel about being pregnant?"

She drew a deep breath and let it out. "At first, I panicked. Now that I've had a couple of days to accept the reality, I'm still scared, but I want the baby."

He released a breath he hadn't been aware of holding, and his shoulders eased down. "Okay, good. That's good." He'd barely processed the news, but he couldn't imagine any other outcome. He'd have let her decide. After all, it was her body. But he was relieved.

"You're okay with that?" Her hand gripped his.

He nodded. "I am. But we have a lot more to talk about, yes?"

"Yes."

And he'd lead her through it until he knew everything.

A knock sounded on the door and they turned.

"Are you ready for dinner?" Maggie asked, placing the bottle of beer on a coaster on the table by the sofa.

"We need some time, Maggie. But thank you. We'll come in when we're ready," Jade said.

The middle-aged woman smiled. "Of course." She turned and walked away.

Knox shifted to get more comfortable and then faced Jade again. "Okay, so you found out you were pregnant and you ran." Which seemed to be her MO, he realized, thinking back to the morning after their first night together, when she'd planned on sneaking out. "Why?"

She met his gaze. "I didn't know how you'd take the news, for one thing. And then I had my anxiety to consider. I'm on medication, and I need to know what I should discontinue, what I can stay on, and how those answers will impact the baby and me. I was overwhelmed by it all."

Her answers took him off guard, but he internalized his concern. "I don't want you to suffer. We'll find out together and deal with it," he assured her.

Her eyes were wide and he wasn't sure if she believed him. They'd get there, too. "What else?" he asked.

"My birth mother." Her voice was soft, and he knew they'd come to the core of her fear. "When I was eight, I was reading a book in a little nook I loved in the family room. If you didn't know I was there, you wouldn't ever notice me. My brothers came in, talking."

She ran her tongue over her lower lip. "Harrison had been going through a tough time at school. I wouldn't say he was depressed, but some kids were jerks because he liked theater and not sports. And I guess he was thinking about our real mom. And he was telling our other brothers he was worried that one day he'd do what she did."

He winced and wasn't sure what to say.

She continued, so he didn't have to find the words. "Asher, who was fifteen at the time, slapped Harrison on the back and told him he wouldn't inherit her illness because he wasn't a girl. Harrison felt better and the boys went to the kitchen to snack."

"Shit," he muttered.

"Yep." She wriggled, trying to stand.

He shook his head. "Nope. You're here until we're finished."

"I just wanted to pace." She pouted and he found it cute but he refused to give in.

"And I want you close. Go on," he said softly.

She sighed. "Asher's words scared me so badly I got my first migraine that night. I think I worked myself up so much that my body needed to let it out."

"Makes sense. Did you tell anyone what you'd

heard?"

She shook her head. "I was eight. I didn't want to get my brothers in trouble or make anyone mad at me."

"So you internalized what Asher said, even though it was totally incorrect?" Asher would hate himself if he knew what his throwaway comment had done to the sister he loved.

She lifted her shoulders and lowered them again. "I was eight," she repeated. "By the time I learned the truth about heredity and mental illness, migraines were a part of my life. They probably would have been anyway, since they can be inherited. My mother had them, too."

"When did your anxiety surface?" he asked.

"I'm not sure I knew what the feeling was at first. Butterflies in my stomach over nothing in particular. Panicked feelings for no reason. Over-reaction to little arguments with friends that shouldn't have gotten me so agitated. By middle school, I was in the throes of it. Dad took me to a therapist, and that's when I learned I wouldn't inherit Mom's specific mental illness just because I was a girl. The doctor taught me that my issues were my own. But by then, the fear was already deeply ingrained."

"Was that the first time you had therapy?" Knox asked.

She nodded.

It had been a little too late to help, Knox thought, but he knew Michael Dare had been overwhelmed by life and his children when his wife had left, then passed away. He'd done the best he could at the time.

Knox thought back to what Jade had told him about her mother, her desire to be pregnant because she loved the attention, and how she'd neglected the kids she already had. It wasn't a big leap to realize what was really scaring Jade.

"Despite therapy, when you realized you were pregnant, you wondered if your mother's illness would somehow surface in you?"

"Wow. You're smart," she murmured.

He grinned despite the seriousness of the subject. "And that's a good thing for our kid. He or she will have two smart parents." He'd had no idea how much she held inside and suffered with, and he tried to lighten the mood with his words.

She smiled and he was pleased. "Do I know everything now?" he asked.

She met his gaze and nodded. "You do."

"Do you feel any better?"

She lifted her shoulders. "I'm not sure."

He needed to try a different way to reach her. "How are you feeling, then?" She'd been holding his hand, and he managed to switch their positions so he could run his thumb over her skin.

She tipped her head from side to side, stretching her muscles. "Like I want to run away and not have to think about anything. Except it always follows me."

"It?"

"The anxiety and, in this case, my situation." She freed one hand and placed it over her belly.

He'd been expecting that kind of answer. "Okay, first, it's *our* situation. Second? Neither one of us is running away. We can't deal with the future if we're running from the past."

"Have you always been so wise?" she asked.

"It comes with age." He laughed and so did she, breaking the tension that had been hovering around them.

Knowing that, even without the pregnancy, she'd been relationship-shy, he kept quiet about their current status as a couple. As much as he'd planned to come down here and tell her how he felt about her, he now worried about her reaction. Considering the two broken engagements behind her, two men who'd gotten close to her because they'd wanted something, he felt that saying *I love you* now was the worst thing he could do. She'd turn things around in her head and think he was saying it because she was pregnant.

Which meant he was at a loss. Not only did he need to process the fact that he was going to be a father and his life was about to change, but also, the mother of his child had trust issues a mile long. Probably longer.

He had to take a step back and think. Regroup. Figure out what he wanted and what Jade needed. So he asked the only thing he could think of.

"How about we go eat dinner?"

She blinked at him in surprise but nodded. "Yes. Good idea."

He slid away from her and gave them both room to stand up and stretch after their long talk. He followed her out of the library and toward the veranda, where they would be eating.

Knox knew he needed a plan, but the only thing he could come up with was to back off and let them process the news together. The heavy conversation ought to end. If he could convince her to stay on the island with him and enjoy their time together, he could remind her of how good things were between them. And Jade would relax before they had to return to New York and deal with their new reality.

After that? One step at a time.

During dinner, Jade picked at her food, and there wasn't much in the way of conversation, nor could he manage to engage her. Without warning, she rose and made a sudden dash inside the house. Knox rushed after her and found her in the nearest bathroom, leaning over the toilet.

He stepped out to give her privacy, returning when he heard the flush. He stepped back in as she rose to her feet. She turned on the faucets, leaning over the sink to splash her face.

Wanting to help, Knox gathered her hair in his hand, making it easier for her to wash up. She finished and patted her face with a towel.

"Are you okay?" he asked, feeling useless and unable to do anything but stand by her side.

"Yeah. But I need to brush my teeth." She turned away from him, and he followed her to the bedroom, waiting outside the bathroom while she finished up.

When she walked out, her face was makeup free, and though she'd been out in the sun today, her skin appeared washed out. He sat down on the mattress and patted the space beside him.

She lowered herself to the bed. "Welcome to paradise," she said with a shake of her head.

He let out a laugh. "At least you can make jokes."

"What else can I do?" She shrugged. "Did you eat enough dinner? You can go back and finish… Or did I ruin your appetite?" She winced, wrinkling her nose at the thought.

"I'm fine." He placed his hand on the back of her neck and rubbed his thumb back and forth against her soft skin. "How about you? Feeling any better?"

"Yes."

He brushed her hair back from her face with his free hand. "Why don't you lie down? Tomorrow we can spend the day on the beach. If you want to talk, we'll talk. If you'd rather relax in silence, that's okay, too. But I do have one question."

She glanced up at him and raised her eyebrows.

"Have you been to a doctor?"

She shook her head. "Not yet."

"Then that's the first thing on the agenda when we get back. Can we agree on that?"

Her fingers curled into the bedspread. "Yes. We're agreed."

He relaxed, knowing she'd be taken care of. "Now for however long we stay in paradise, we enjoy."

Chapter Nine

J ADE HAD AGREED to spend three days on the island and during their time there, he learned more about her. She loved the beach and curling her toes in the sand. She preferred the shade of an umbrella to direct sunlight beating down on her skin. He already knew her choice of reading was romance, because she loved the fact that the right couple ended up together, something that gave him hope. Jade might claim to be finished with relationships, but she was a woman who longed for her own happily-ever-after. And Knox wanted to give it to her.

While she'd napped on the lounge earlier—a double lounger that had miraculously shown up his second day here—he thought about what he could do to make their last night special. Thanks to her pregnancy, fish had been off the menu since he'd arrived. She couldn't look at it without getting sick. They'd had their share of chicken and steak, and he doubted she wanted to go to a restaurant where she might or might not enjoy the meal or need to excuse herself suddenly.

He'd noted that she did well when she ate carbs, so

he asked the chef to make them waffles for dinner. Afterwards, he'd give her the choice of driving into Eleuthera to walk around or going downstairs to the home theater and watching a movie. Since Asher's villa felt like it existed on an island of its own, it was hard to remember there was another world with restaurants, stores, hotels, and people less than five miles away.

What Knox came up with might not be an expensive dinner out but at least he'd taken Jade's needs into consideration. From what she'd told him, that was something neither Theo nor her previous ex had ever done.

He lay back in his chaise and glanced over. Jade was still asleep, her lips slightly parted. A drop of sweat glistened on her chest, and he watched as it dripped into her cleavage displayed by the bikini he'd cajoled her into wearing again. He shifted in his seat, but his erection wouldn't let him get comfortable and he groaned.

At the unintentional sound, her eyelids fluttered open and her gaze met his. She blinked and pushed herself to a sitting position. "Oh, wow. How long did I sleep?"

"An hour. Are you thirsty? Someone brought out some ice, bottled sodas, and water." Asher had an excellent staff, and Knox had no doubt it was because he treated them well.

She nodded. "Some water would be great."

He scooped some ice, then poured water into a plastic cup and handed it to Jade. She took a long sip and let out a moan. "That's so good." She placed the cup against her chest, no doubt to cool herself off.

"You're killing me here." He adjusted himself without shame.

When they'd decided to stay on the island, they hadn't discussed sleeping together. But they'd climbed into the same bed that night. She'd fallen asleep first, and when he woke up, she was wrapped around him, her nipples pressed against his chest, her sex rubbing against his cock.

Their eyes had locked and they'd silently agreed as to what came next. Once they'd undressed, she looked up at him with trust in her eyes and told him they didn't need condoms if he was sure he was clean. She'd been tested after Theo, and she hadn't been with anyone since. Except him. Knox had had a recent physical. She believed him and he knew what that trust cost her to give. It meant everything to him.

"Is something bothering you?" she asked with a smile lifting her lips.

Her flirty tone boded well for him. "I take it you're feeling okay?"

She rose and straddled him on the chair. "I am and I plan on taking advantage of the moment."

He grasped her hips, pushing her onto his dick.

"Mmm." She rocked against him, and he held on to her waist as she picked up a rhythm that worked for her.

He gritted his teeth and held back the need to rip off their clothes or thrust up and take his own pleasure. He needed to watch her own hers first. She was so damned sexy, taking what she needed until her orgasm hit. She threw her head back and rode him, grinding herself against him, his name on her lips.

By the time she came down from the high, he thought he'd explode. She climbed off him on shaky legs and pulled off her bikini bottoms, leaving her naked from the waist down.

He rose and stripped off his board shorts, then stretched back out on the lounge. "Climb on," he said, barely recognizing his deep voice.

Her gaze darkened and she did as he asked, putting a knee on either side of his hips. She grabbed his erection in her hand and ran it up and down his shaft before settling the head between her thighs.

They locked gazes as she lowered herself, her eyes dilating, and she took him inside her.

He groaned, lost in the best possible way. She clasped him in warmth and squeezed her inner walls around him, her every move perfection.

She lifted up and dropped herself down, rocking

forward each time their bodies connected. "I don't expect to come again," she said. "It's your turn."

He raised his eyebrows. "Have I ever left you hanging?"

She laughed. "No, but that doesn't mean I think it'll be every time."

He wasn't amused, nor did he want to think about her past disappointments. "When you're with me, you come. And this time it'll be while I'm inside you. Okay?"

At his words, her expression softened. "Okay."

He clasped their hands together, and though she did her share of the work, he lifted his hips and thrust up, joining their bodies and bringing them both higher every time.

He didn't expect to last long, not with her sweet pussy squeezing him tight, but he felt the tingle even faster than he'd anticipated.

"Come for me, beautiful." He released her hand and slid his finger back and forth over her clit.

"Oh my God. Don't stop." She stilled, her body stiff as he rubbed twice more and she began to shake and tremble around him. He felt every quake of her body and he thrust up and into her. His orgasm hit hard and he came harder, his climax pushing her into another one that had her falling on top of him, their sweaty bodies sticking together.

He wrapped an arm around her back as they caught their breath.

She rolled off him with a groan. "Sex in the heat and humidity is great in the moment. Not so amazing after." She laughed as she grabbed a towel.

After they'd cleaned up as well as they could and dressed again, she lay back against the lounge. Throughout their days here, he'd kept his focus on Jade. It was time for him to give her another reminder.

He rolled to his side and placed his hand on her still-flat stomach where their baby grew. "As unexpected as this is, I'm glad it's happening with you."

She turned her head to face him. "Really?"

He loved her. Was this the right time to say so? Would she believe him? He moved in closer. "Really, Jade. I love you."

Her eyes filled and she swallowed.

He didn't expect her to say it back, but the fact that she was here and not running? He considered that a huge win. And he was a man who counted wins.

She reached over and slipped her hand in his, and it was enough. For now.

★ ★ ★

WHEN THEY BOARDED Asher's plane the next day, Jade was still reeling from hearing those three little words come from Knox. *I love you.* They'd been said to

196

her before, but never with such intensity or passion. She knew how special Knox was, and it had been on the tip of her tongue to say the words back. But he deserved to hear them when they came free from baggage.

For the first time, she believed she might be on her way.

She glanced at Knox as he hooked his seat belt beside her.

Noticing her staring, he grinned and treated her to a wink that had her stomach turning over in a wonderful way. She was grateful for their three glorious days on the island. With no one to bother them, she'd gotten to know Knox better. The patience she'd seen him display with his sister was truly a part of him, and he extended it to the way he treated her. It made her more certain that, for the first time, she'd picked a good man.

No man had ever planned a meal around her and her needs. Their last night had been fun, and despite her nausea, she'd enjoyed bites of the unexpected waffles and the ice cream that had followed.

As she buckled her own seat belt, she thought about the lifestyle changes she'd need to make and the people she'd have to tell about her pregnancy. That thought sent her stomach from good churning to nervous roiling.

As if he sensed something was wrong, Knox grasped her hand and squeezed tight. She smiled to reassure him, then shut her eyes for takeoff. She fell asleep and didn't wake up until the pilot let them know they were starting their descent.

"Almost there," Knox said.

She nodded. "Did I mention Asher is meeting us at the airport?" She hadn't been able to talk her brother out of his plan, despite her best efforts.

"Of course he is," Knox said. To her surprise, he let out a low chuckle. "We need to tell him and the rest of your family about the baby. Not to mention Holly."

Jade didn't want to insult him, but she'd given this some thought and bit down on her lower lip before filling him in. "I was hoping I could do that myself. I don't think it's fair to subject you to the firing squad."

"Do you think I'd let you face them without me?" He threaded their fingers together.

If he meant to reassure her, his insistence did the opposite. "I'm not sure I'm ready to see Asher and Zach make a mess of your handsome face." Though she tried to make light of the subject, she wasn't kidding.

Nick and Harrison were more likely to deal with Knox using their words. But her older two brothers were better with their fists. And her father? She winced just thinking about him finding out his daughter was unmarried and pregnant by Asher's close friend.

"You think I'm handsome?" Knox treated her to his sexiest grin, making her both laugh and roll her eyes. Of course he'd pick out that part of her statement.

"I promise I can handle anything your brothers dish out. Now relax while we land. I'll handle everything," he said.

"Right. I'll let the big, strong man fight my battles," she muttered. From the moment she'd found out she was pregnant, she'd let her thoughts and her life spiral.

Well, no longer. She'd run off to the island to wrap her head around the changes to come, and she felt strong enough now to handle things herself. If Knox thought she'd allow him to make their decisions and control her, he had a lot to learn about Jade Dare.

The plane landed. They gathered their bags and the door opened. Knox stepped out first, turning to take her hand so he could help her down the steps and onto the tarmac. He was a gentleman, and she couldn't complain about that part of his personality.

They met up with Asher by his car. He immediately pulled her into a long, brotherly hug—one she needed.

"Tell me you're okay," he said as he stepped back to study her.

"I am, just like I told you every day when I called you as promised." She kissed his cheek. "Thanks for worrying. But I'm good."

Asher looked over her shoulder at Knox, her brother's worried expression turning into more of a scowl, lips turned down, eyebrows, too.

Jade poked Asher in his side. "Cut it out. Knox took good care of me."

Instead of being reassured, Asher's frown grew fiercer. "I don't want to know how."

"Eew! Stop!"

Knox stepped forward and extended his hand until Asher had no choice but to accept.

"There. That wasn't so hard, was it?" Jade asked. "You told him where I was and arranged for the jet to take him there. So what's your problem now?"

"I feel like something's going on, and I want to know what it is." Asher's gaze darted from Jade to Knox and back again.

"We'll talk in private," she said.

Knox cleared his throat. "Actually, I thought we could all sit down and have an adult conversation."

Jade closed her eyes, counted to five, then opened them again. She didn't have time to go for ten. She turned to Knox. "I told you I'd like to discuss this with my brother. Alone."

Frowning again, Asher held up both hands in a *stop* gesture. "As it happens, the family is at Serenity and Dad's house. They expect me to bring you home to see them. Then we can go back to the city."

"*Why?*" she asked.

"Really? You ghosted them. We're not the kind of family that goes without talking and texting almost daily." He had a point. They had group chats for different types of things. Jade, Nick, and Michael for business, the whole family for check-ins and family gatherings, etc.

She swallowed hard. "How many of them are there?"

"All of them." Asher folded his arms across his chest, looking smug.

Knox stepped closer to her and whispered in her ear. "No running. Not from them and especially not from me. We don't want this to turn into a game of hide-and-seek."

She stiffened at his reminder.

"And Jade?" he asked.

She met his serious gaze and looked into his handsome, tanned face. "I will *always* find you."

Something about the way he said that sent tremors of awareness oozing through her veins, much the way arousal did when his lips traveled over her body. That was something he'd done often while they'd been alone on the island. He hadn't had to talk her into anything sexually. They were already sharing a bed. It made sense for them to be together. Especially the first morning, when she'd woken up entangled in his arms, chest to chest, her cheek against his, her body wrapped around him like a spider monkey. With her being pregnant and them both having been tested recently, sex without a condom had been natural as he'd slid into her wet heat.

"I don't want to know where you just went in your head or why your cheeks are red and flushed," Asher muttered. "Can we make a decision? Who's coming to Greenwich?"

Jade made the mistake of looking at Knox, who grinned, then winked at her.

Asher groaned.

And Jade's face flamed redder. "Fine! Let's all go!" She raised her arms and gestured to the waiting car, eager to end the embarrassment.

She walked toward the limousine, head high, knowing she'd rather face the guillotine than announce to her entire family that she was pregnant... and Knox was the father.

JADE HAD SET her jaw and didn't speak on the ride to

her parents' house, so Asher and Knox picked up the slack. Ignoring the elephant in the back of the car—Knox's relationship with Jade—they talked about the upcoming training camp in August and the Warriors' prospects for making it to the postseason, despite it being so early in the football year.

Jade stared out the tinted window, and Knox put a hand on her leg, above her knee, and kept it there as he and Asher spoke. Other than an eyebrow lift and a partial glare, Asher didn't mention it. He might as well set the stage for what was to come, Knox thought.

After a traffic-filled ride, they wound their way around tree-lined streets with the houses too far back from the road to be visible. The driver turned and the car pulled into a long driveway. A variety of expensive vehicles were parked, backing up what Asher had said. The entire family was waiting for them.

Knox knew he ought to be nervous, but the only people whose opinions mattered to him were Jade's parents, and that was where he kept his focus. Approaching them after getting their daughter pregnant showed a lack of respect, and though he wasn't sorry he and Jade were having a baby, he wished things hadn't played out this way. Still, if it bound Jade to him and gave him a better shot at convincing her to be his, he'd work with it.

As the car shut off, Jade stiffened beside him. "Relax," he whispered to her.

She treated him to an unladylike snort. "I didn't plan on the whole family being here when I told my parents the news."

Asher raised an eyebrow. "What news?"

"Let's just go," she muttered and leaned forward so the driver could help her out. Knox and Asher followed.

Michael and Serenity Dare were waiting at the front door for them. Jade hugged Serenity, then her dad, apologizing for disappearing on them.

"I understand Asher knew where you were and that you wanted to be by yourself, but next time, can you just let us hear your voice so we don't worry?" Serenity, an attractive woman with raven-colored hair that hung to her shoulders, said.

"I will," Jade promised.

"There won't be a next time," Knox said.

At his pronouncement, three sets of eyes turned his way. Thank God the rest of the family was somewhere else in the house, he thought, realizing he'd opened up the conversation Jade wasn't ready for.

Sure enough, she glared at him.

"What does that mean?" Michael asked.

Since Knox and Asher had gone to business school together and had been friends for years, Knox knew Michael. He even called him by his first name.

"Knox means I promised I wouldn't run again if something upsets me. I'll stay and talk things out," Jade said, jumping in to explain.

"What's going on? I feel like you all know something that we don't." Michael put an arm around his wife's shoulder and pulled her closer.

"Not *everyone* is clued in," Asher said, still giving Knox a death stare.

Michael's expression grew darker and his eyes narrowed. "Someone better explain."

From being calm and certain he could handle telling Jade's father he'd knocked up his daughter—though not in those words—Knox took another look at the man and broke into a sweat.

"I'd like your permission to marry Jade," he blurted out, the words true but not the ones he'd planned on saying.

"What?" All four people, Michael, Serenity, Asher *and Jade*, spoke at once. But it was only Jade who Knox was concerned about, and she was not happy.

Arms folded across her chest, her eyes all but shooting daggers at him, she shook her head. "No, that's not what he meant to say. Mom, Dad, Asher…" She drew in a deep breath. "I'm pregnant and Knox is the father."

"What?" Her father stepped forward, and she held up a hand because she obviously wasn't finished.

"We haven't decided how to handle things, but we are not getting married just because I'm having his baby. However, *I am keeping him. Or her.*" Her hands came to rest on her belly, something he enjoyed watching her do.

"Holy shit," Layla said, walking ahead of the rest of the family, who had chosen that moment to join them from the other side of the house.

"Watch your mouth, young lady," Serenity said.

"But she's right. Holy shit." That came from one of the triplets. Knox had never been able to tell them apart, and at the moment, it didn't matter.

Michael ran a hand over his lightly graying hair. "Kids, out. Layla, go to your room and FaceTime with a friend. Boys, go outside and shoot hoops or something."

Grumbling, the kids dispersed.

"Can we talk?" Michael asked Knox.

His heart skipped a beat, but before he could answer, Jade spoke.

"Oh, no. This is not the dark ages. You two don't need to have a private conversation about me, my body, my choices, or some marriage we never even discussed!" Her voice rose along with her anger.

Knox put a hand on her back, hoping to calm her. He didn't want her upset.

"Umm, Aurora, Leah, and I are going to go

home," Nick said. "You don't need an audience. But Jade? Call me," her twin said. "Say bye, Leah."

The adorable little girl hugged her grandparents, aunts, and uncles, then stopped at Jade. "Auntie Jade?"

"Yes, sweetie?" Jade knelt down in front of her niece.

"You call me, too," Leah ordered.

Everyone laughed, breaking the tension. "I will," Jade promised. "Now give me a hug."

Leah wrapped her arms around Jade's neck, then finally Nick and Aurora said their goodbyes and herded Leah out the front door.

Harrison cleared his throat. "I'll leave, too, but we'll talk." His warning gaze held Knox's before he strode out.

Zach stepped forward next. "I know where to bury bodies," he said before slapping Knox on the back.

"Cut it out," Jade muttered.

Chuckling, Zach took off.

That left only her parents and one sibling for Knox to deal with. He knew better than to think Asher would leave.

"Can we at least take this into the family room?" Serenity asked. Without waiting for a reply, she walked through the open-concept layout, toward the huge room with an oversized sofa and chairs to hold their large family.

Serenity clearly expected everyone to follow and they did. Michael settled into a seat beside his wife. Asher sat across the way in a club chair. Knox waited for Jade to sit, but she remained standing.

"Knox, have a seat."

She waited for him to do as she said before she faced her family. "I have something to say to all of you." She paused a beat. "Maybe I shouldn't have taken off when I found out I was pregnant, but I needed time to process the news. And now I want to make a few things clear."

Knox appreciated the way she'd taken control, and he let her handle her own family. He'd be here for backup, if needed.

"We're listening, honey." Serenity's warm gaze settled on her daughter.

Jade nodded. "I'm twenty-six years old. This may not be how I envisioned my life going, but things happen that change our path. Knox wants to be a part of the baby's life, and what happens next is up to us."

He wondered if she realized her hands, once again, protectively cupped her stomach as she spoke. He loved this fierce part of her he'd never seen before. She'd be a damned good mother, not that he'd had any doubts.

Jade cleared her throat. "I love you all and I came here to tell you the news, but I don't need you to solve my problems for me. And that includes you." She pointed to Knox. "As gallant as it is to ask for my father's permission to marry me, this isn't a typical situation, and it's something you and I should have discussed first."

He let her continue since she had a point. Despite thinking he knew what to do, he'd panicked and hadn't handled this meeting well.

"So you aren't getting married?" Asher asked, his pissed-off stare on Knox again. "Because it would be the right thing to do."

Jade wrinkled her nose. "In what century? I already said we will not be getting married just because I'm having his baby."

Ouch, Knox thought. What about marrying for love? He loved her. He'd told her as much. But he knew that if he'd uttered the words *before* she'd revealed she was pregnant, he'd have a better chance at convincing her to marry him than he did now. Still, he wasn't a man who gave up when things got rough.

Michael rose to his feet. "I understand. You two deserve to work things out together." He nodded at Knox, then held out his arms.

Jade walked over, stepping into her father's embrace. "We're here for you," he said. "Whatever you need."

"Thank you," she said, stepping back to hug Serenity.

Asher rose to his feet. "I just want you to be happy." He, too, got in a quick squeeze around her shoulders.

"Umm, I have something else I need you to know so… can you all sit back down?" Jade asked, taking everyone by surprise.

Even Knox wasn't sure what there was left to discuss, but he did as she asked and waited, along with the others, to find out.

Chapter Ten

WITH ASHER AND her parents in one place, it was time to have the serious conversation Jade had been avoiding since she was a child. Knox had stressed the importance of not running from her problems, and Jade was taking it seriously.

For this talk, she wanted to be sitting down. Once settled, she clasped Knox's hand in hers for support. He held on tight.

"What's going on?" Asher leaned forward, concern in his expression. It was better than the anger he'd shown earlier, but she was going to hurt him, and she didn't want him to blame himself.

"While on the island, Knox and I were talking, and some things came up that I never told you." She slid her tongue over her bottom lip. "Remember when I was a kid, how I used to read in that huge Queen Anne chair in the library?"

Her mom laughed. "Sometimes I couldn't find you, and eventually, I learned to check there first."

Jade smiled. "One afternoon, I was curled up there, reading. I was eight. And the boys were walking past, heading to the kitchen."

Asher tipped his head to the side. She could almost see the wheels turning while he tried to come up with what she was going to say. "That was back when Harrison was having a hard time at school because he was into theater." She drew a deep breath. "I heard him tell you"—she looked at Asher—"that he was worried. That because he was depressed, he was afraid he'd do to himself what Mom did."

Serenity gasped. Obviously, Harrison hadn't shared those fears with her. Her father's eyes grew wide. He, too, appeared stunned. But Asher just grew pale. Without a doubt, he remembered what he'd told their sibling.

"Jade?" Serenity pressed for more.

Jade swallowed hard. "I… ummm…" She didn't know how to say it.

"I told Harrison he wouldn't inherit Mom's illness because he wasn't a girl." Asher ran a hand through his hair and groaned.

"I got my first migraine that night," Jade said softly.

Rising from his seat, Asher began to pace. "I just wanted to reassure him. I figured if I took away the possibility, Harrison would forget about it. I mean, what did I know? I was a teenager and busy with my own problems. But I never would have said anything if

I'd known you were there. Shit." He rubbed his palms against his eyes, his self-recrimination as bad as she'd figured it would be.

Jade released Knox's hand and jumped up, standing in Asher's path. "I know you didn't realize I was there. That's why I never told anyone. I knew how badly you would feel. It wasn't until the anxiety started in middle school and I went to therapy that I found out the truth. Sure, I could inherit mental illness, but my issues weren't presenting anything like our birth mother's. This isn't your fault." She touched Asher's shoulder and he managed a nod.

"Jesus Christ. I did a shit job of taking care of you kids after your mother left. I should have gotten you all help sooner." Her father bowed his head. "My emotions were all over the place, and there were five of you, all different ages. I was in over my head."

Serenity wrapped her arm around him. "We all did the best we could at the time. I'm sorry I didn't ask more questions or think of pushing for therapy. I just wanted to get Jade's migraines treated so the pain would go away. It never dawned on me there was an inciting cause."

"Serenity, you were their nanny. It was my responsibility to see what my kids needed and I failed," Michael said.

Jade glanced at Knox, who remained silent while

the family worked out their past. He was a steadying force, and she was grateful to have him by her side.

"Nobody failed," Jade said. "Nobody is to blame. It was time for me to tell you, but not because I want anyone beating themselves up over something that happened a long time ago."

"Jade, honey, why did this come up for you again now?" Serenity asked.

She walked back to Knox and lowered herself onto the cushion beside him. She knew she had to face this, too. "I just want to be a good mother. Unlike… Audrey." Jade refused to give her birth parent the label that Serenity had earned. Though she wished things had been different, she was grateful for all the good people in her life. Especially the woman who'd raised her, whose eyes were now damp.

"I want you to listen to me," Serenity said. "Asher, you, too."

He turned toward his stepmother, his expression still ravaged with guilt.

"Audrey suffered with tremendous pain and emotional turmoil. I didn't know her well, but despite her lack of attentiveness, she loved her babies." Serenity rubbed her hands on her silk pants, her nerves showing.

Michael stopped the movement by threading his fingers with hers.

"I feel guilty, too," Serenity went on. "Because I got to raise you all. I fell in love with all of Audrey's children. I have my family because she is gone." Serenity drew in a trembling breath. "Your father is right. We all needed therapy." She sniffed and blinked back her tears.

Jade's heart hurt for everyone in this room.

Serenity glanced around, meeting both Jade and Asher's gazes. "I want you both to let your anger at Audrey—and at yourselves—go. Let the worry go, too. Do whatever you need to do in order to come to terms with the past. Get help, talk to whoever makes you feel better. But know this—Audrey didn't leave you because she chose to. She left because she wanted her suffering to end."

The lump in Jade's throat had grown so large she didn't know if she could hold back the tears much longer.

"And you." Serenity's dark eyes pinned her in place. "You are the most compassionate, warm, giving woman I know. And I'm absolutely certain you will be an amazing mother. You will be present. You'll enjoy every moment. So please don't torture yourself with something that will never happen."

"I agree," Knox whispered, obviously not wanting to intrude on a family moment.

They went through the round of hugs and tears

again and came away with a new understanding of the past and each other. And Jade promised herself to think about everything Serenity had said and to get help if she felt this conversation hadn't done enough to heal her.

Not long after, everyone said their goodbyes. The ride home with Asher and Knox was quiet, each of them lost in thought. Asher had the driver stop at Jade's apartment first, and Knox insisted on getting out with her.

They said goodbye to her brother, and Knox walked her upstairs, leaving his suitcase with the doorman so he could grab it on his way out again. She wasn't sure how she felt about him not asking to stay over, but she couldn't deny she needed time to think.

He escorted her to her door and she let them both inside. He carried her suitcase into her room and laid it on the bed, making it easier for her to unpack later. In silence, they walked back through the hall and toward the front door.

Exhaustion had caught up with her and she yawned. "Today was a day," she said with a shake of her head. "Does every conversation have to be so long and draining?"

Knox treated her to a warm smile, which, of course, she found sexy. "Dealing with the past isn't easy, but you're getting through it."

"Who knew finding out I was pregnant would bring up all these old issues?" she murmured.

"You're strong and everything will work out." He braced his hands on either side of her face. "Don't think for one minute that I don't want to stay with you tonight. But I have to go home, unpack, and be at work early tomorrow. Besides, I'm pretty sure you need time to unwind and process what happened today."

"I do." Then why was she so sad he was leaving?

He dipped his head and pressed their mouths together in a kiss that was gentle but sensual at the same time. His lips slid over hers, back and forth, until his tongue slipped inside and tangled with hers. She wrapped her arms around his neck, pulling him closer as she moaned into his mouth. A tremor shook his body, and he deepened the connection, one hand now cupping the back of her neck as the kiss went on and on.

Finally, he lifted his head. "If we don't stop, I won't be able to leave," he said in a gruff voice.

It was on the tip of her tongue to tell him not to go, but she knew he was right. A lot of issues had come up today, and she needed to give them time to settle.

For that to happen, she needed quiet time. A warm bath, a cup of hot tea. "Okay," she agreed at last.

He rubbed his nose alongside hers. "Get some rest."

With the way her body was vibrating and her sex pulsing with need, she doubted sleep would come. But she grudgingly let Knox out and locked up behind him.

And though she'd intended to think about the things Serenity had said, her mind went to Knox instead. He'd never brought up the subject of marriage until he mentioned it to her father. Surely if that was something he wanted, he would have discussed it with her when they were alone.

Was he giving her time after the trauma of her family meeting? Or had he changed his mind altogether? Worse, had it been an impulsive question he was grateful she'd shut down?

And considering the negative gut reaction she'd had at the time, why was she so disappointed now?

★　★　★

THE NEXT MORNING, Knox walked into the stadium and immediately went into action, attending consecutive meetings he'd rescheduled during his time away. By the time he returned to his office, it was long after lunchtime and his stomach was growling.

He picked up his cell to order in, but a knock stopped him. "Come in."

"Hi!" Holly opened the door, then walked over and gave him a hug. "I missed you."

"I missed you, too."

She shoved his shoulder with her hand. "Next time you disappear, I expect more than *'Don't worry, took a quick trip, I'll be back. Hold down the fort.'*" She quoted his text message to her.

"I'm sorry. But you did a great job." He strode past her and shut the door so they had privacy. "I have news and you might want to sit down to hear it."

She swept her hand over the back of her skirt and lowered herself into a chair, crossing her legs in front of her.

"Ready?" He drew a deep breath. "Jade is pregnant and I'm the father."

"Aaah!" She let out a scream and jumped to her feet. "You aren't joking, are you?"

He shook his head. "I'm going to be a father."

Holly's eyes grew wide. "Are you… happy about it?"

He'd spent so much time worrying about Jade and her reactions, he'd pushed his feelings into the background. He met his sister's gaze. "I wasn't expecting the news, but once I wrapped my head around it, yeah, I'm happy. And nervous."

Holly smiled. "You are going to be a great dad. You're already an amazing brother." She hugged him tight. "How is Jade?"

How *was* Jade? "Shaken up but adjusting."

Holly nodded. "Any plans?" She wriggled her eyebrows and nudged him with her shoulder. "Like moving in together or getting married?"

"Okay, little troublemaker. Promise me you're going to stay out of it. Let Jade and me figure out what we want, in our own way, and in our own time."

Holly nodded and raised a hand. "I swear. I'm just so excited! I'm going to be an aunt!"

He laughed. "You are. And you'll be a good one."

"Can I tell Miles?" she asked.

He nodded. "Of course." He wouldn't expect her to keep secrets from her fiancé.

"Thank you."

He strode over to his desk and began looking through the notes of phone calls he'd received, noticing Holly had left messages with his secretary. Often. "You wanted to talk to me about something?"

She shook her head and laughed. "You weren't returning my calls. Yes, I wanted to talk, but it's not about business."

He had a hunch it wasn't wedding-related and raised an eyebrow. "What's going on?"

"Theo wants to have lunch. He said he knows he's been a jerk, and he wants to make it up to me. And with the wedding in less than six months, I just want peace. So don't be angry at me if I go. Okay?" Holly's cheeks flushed and she couldn't meet his gaze.

Knox shook his head and groaned. "All I can do is tell you what I think. I won't be mad at you, no matter what you decide." With Holly's mother long gone and her father deceased, his sister was desperate for family, and fucking Theo was playing on that weakness—again.

She twisted her hands in front of her, her nerves showing. "You don't think I should see him."

He blew out a long breath. "I think Theo always has a reason for what he does, and it usually benefits him. But you have to do what you need to do."

She nodded. "Thanks."

That probably meant she would meet up with her brother, despite Knox's warning. "Just be careful, okay?"

"I will."

After she'd walked out, he felt bad, knowing Holly would be upset that Knox didn't approve of her having anything to do with Theo. Knox didn't want to control her, but he just needed her to be aware that Theo always had an agenda. And he wouldn't hesitate to use Holly if it furthered his plans.

But Knox had warned her. That was all he could do.

He settled in behind his desk, ordered in lunch,

and confirmed times for meetings that had been moved because of his unexpected trip. Tonight, he had dinner plans with his general manager, Steve Powell, to discuss his frustrations with the power dynamic within the front office.

When his cell rang, interrupting his thoughts, he was surprised to see Jade's name on the screen. He'd been planning to call her once he'd caught up on work, before he went out for the evening.

He tapped the phone and answered. "Jade, hi. How are you feeling?"

"Okay. I only got sick once today so far, but I'm always queasy."

He winced. "I'm sorry. Is there anything I can bring you?"

"No, thanks. So... the reason I'm calling is, I asked Aurora about her ob-gyn. They were booked solid, but she pulled strings and got me in at the end of this week."

Relief washed over him. "That's good." It was early in her pregnancy, but he'd feel better knowing everything she was experiencing was normal and that she and the baby were okay. "When is the appointment?"

"Friday at eleven. But don't worry. I know you're probably busy after being away. Lauren said she'd go with me and I'll let you know how it goes." She spoke quickly, as if, by doing so, he'd just accept what she said.

As if he'd let her go with a friend to *their* first baby appointment. "What's the doctor's address?" he asked. "Or better yet, I'll come pick you up and we can go together. Will you be at the office or are you going straight from home?"

"I… You *want* to come?"

"I'm not sure what there is about *we're in this together* you didn't understand."

Silence greeted him and she let out a sigh. He hoped it was one of relief. "I'll take the morning off. You can come to my apartment. It's closer and easier for you."

He smiled. "Great. I'll be there at ten."

"Okay. Umm, Knox?"

"What is it, beautiful?"

"Thank you."

He closed his eyes and swallowed back any reaction. She didn't need to thank him, nor should she assume he didn't want to be there.

But she definitely needed more proof of his feelings than he'd given her in order for her to have faith in him. And ultimately, in *them*. He considered his options and decided what to do. After making a phone call and setting up an appointment for later this afternoon, he called Asher and asked him to come along. Although Knox knew Holly would have loved to be there, he wanted this to be kept a secret and decided not to tell his exuberant sister ahead of time. Knox loved Holly to death, but she'd been known to let things slip.

A couple of hours later, he and Asher were walking down Fifth Avenue.

"I can't believe I'm doing this," Asher said, as they headed into Harry Winston's, where he had an appointment.

Knox laughed. "Would you rather I left you out of it completely? Let your sister think you still don't approve?"

Asher grumbled but he was here, and that's all Knox cared about.

As they sat with a salesman, looking at rings, Knox shook his head. "None of these jump out at me." They'd already discussed the four C's, and the man knew what Knox was looking for, but the man didn't know *Jade*.

"What do you think?" he asked Asher. "Your sister isn't flashy but she deserves something special. Something with meaning."

"Aah," the salesman said, jumping up. "I have just the thing." The salesman removed the tray in front of Knox and returned with a single ring on a velvet cushion. "A three-carat heart-shaped halo engagement ring surrounded by a bead setting of diamonds and a diamond platinum band."

"This is it." Knox loved it, and more importantly, he thought Jade would, too. "I could go bigger but she's not someone who'd want to walk around with something huge on her finger."

"Agreed," Asher said. "That's very Jade."

"I'm glad you approve," Knox said, unable to withhold a smirk. "I cannot wait until it's your turn."

"Don't hold your breath," Asher muttered.

Knox shook his head. "I'll take it."

"Size?" the man asked.

"Six and a half," he said.

At Asher's raised eyebrows, Knox answered. "Lauren's been shopping with her and she told me." He turned to the salesman. "I'll wait while you size it."

"Of course, Mr. Sinclair." The fact was, money talked, and when he walked out of the store, Knox had the ring in his pocket.

"Do you have a plan?" Asher shoved his hands into his pants pockets.

"Yep." Grinning, Knox climbed into Asher's car.

"Going to tell me?" Asher asked as he slid in behind him and his driver shut the door.

"Nope." Knox laughed. He appreciated his friend's help, but what happened next was between him and Jade.

Leaning back, he patted the box in his pocket. When he got home, he'd put the ring in his safe until he was ready for the big moment.

★　★　★

JADE WALKED OUT of her apartment at seven thirty Thursday morning. She smiled at the doorman and turned right, deciding to walk for a few blocks before hailing a cab for her eight-thirty a.m. appointment with a therapist in Midtown. Jade had gotten a referral from Aurora's psychologist because Jade's doctor only handled medication and light conversation. After her talk with her family, Jade needed more than that.

It would feel good to unburden herself to an unbiased third party. The suppressed anger she held on to about her birth parent and her feelings about becoming a mother weren't healthy. Serenity had a point. These emotions should have been handled earlier. Even Jade's therapy for anxiety hadn't delved that deep.

She glanced up at the blue sky and drew in a breath of morning air, her nerves about the appointment bubbling up. This new psychologist was normally booked, but she'd had a cancellation and been able to fit Jade in this morning. After they met and if they decided they were a good fit, the therapist would work out a more regular schedule.

Jade's parents, as well as Asher and Knox, knew about her decision to get help. They were happy. To her surprise, she'd also shared the news with Holly when she'd called to congratulate Jade about the baby. Somehow, they'd gotten into deeper conversation, and once Jade made the appointment, she'd texted Holly the details because she knew the other woman would understand. Holly's bouncy personality hid a serious girl who possessed a well of understanding about life. She ought to, given her own past.

Holly told Jade that she'd met Theo for lunch this week and had come away disappointed. Holly could use some therapy, too, Jade mused. She needed to talk about losing her parents in different ways and to stop seeking anything from a biological brother incapable of giving love.

Jade knew therapy took time, but just the fact that she was trying to understand her heredity before the baby arrived made her feel like she was already taking steps toward a happier life. Tomorrow was her first ob-gyn appointment, and she was becoming more excited about the baby and less panicked.

The short week since she'd come home from the island had been a good one. Knox called periodically during the day to say hi, and he arrived at her apartment each night after work with takeout dinner in hand. He'd stay to eat and clean up, refusing to let her help, then he'd kiss her until she was vibrating with need and say good night with a gleam in his eyes. The man was up to something. She just didn't know what.

Her cell phone rang and she scrounged through her handbag. Lauren had an early meeting with a new vendor, and Jade wanted to make sure she didn't have any questions.

She pulled out her phone, answering before she glanced at the screen. "Hi," she said, hoping she caught the call before it disconnected.

"Jade? It's Celia."

Jade stood in the middle of the sidewalk, stunned. "Celia? What do you want?" She couldn't imagine she and Knox's ex, the woman who'd slept with Jade's ex-fiancé, had anything to discuss.

"Listen, I know we've had our issues..." Celia said.

"You *think*?"

Celia blew a breath in her ear. "I know. I do. And I'm sorry but I don't have time to explain anything now."

"Then what do you want?"

"If Theo comes by, *do not* go anywhere with him," Celia said, her tone urgent.

Jade narrowed her gaze. "What? Of course I won't go with him. But what are you saying? What do you know?" Before Celia could answer, someone grabbed Jade's wrist and yanked her phone from her hand.

She spun around and came face-to-face with her ex. "Theo?"

He dropped the phone and slammed his shoe heel onto the cell, shattering the screen, before bending to retrieve it and placing it in his pants pocket.

"Theo? What's going on?"

He had the same frenzied look he'd worn that morning he'd come to her apartment and argued with Knox. "Come on, Jade. Let's go." Theo grabbed her forearm and tipped his head toward a row of cars parked behind him.

Her heart picked up speed. "What? No." She tried to wrench free, but he merely tightened his grip and attempted to pull her along with him.

Recalling Celia's warning, she dug in her heels. "I'm not going anywhere with you."

"I just want to talk," he said, facing her, his eyes wild.

Who was this man she no longer recognized? Knox had said Theo was spiraling, and she saw now he was right, making her wonder if she ought to be afraid of him.

"We can talk here," she insisted.

His eyes narrowed. "Damn it, Jade. I don't want to hurt you but you're getting on my nerves." He gripped her arm so tightly she'd be bruised.

He began to pull her down the street, causing her

to trip.

He paused, hauling her to her feet and giving her the chance to kick him in the shin and run.

She didn't get far.

He grabbed her around the waist and pulled her against him. "Stop struggling or I'll hurt you and your baby."

She glanced down to see a small knife he'd obviously been hiding in his hand.

She immediately stilled, fear for the barely there life growing inside her greater than for herself. A quick look around told her the tree-lined side street was empty. There'd be no help coming.

"Fine," she said through clenched teeth. "What do you want from me?"

He seemed to relax, his stance easing, but the knife remained poised in his hand. "I just want us to get into my car, go somewhere, and talk." His hand encircled her wrist, and she let him lead her to a car she didn't recognize. He opened the front passenger door and she climbed in, her pulse racing fast and her gut screaming at her to try and run again.

As if he read her thoughts, he lifted his shirt and revealed a gun in the waistband of his jeans. "I'm going to shut this door and walk around to the driver's side. If you run, I will shoot. And I will aim low. Understand?"

Wrapping her hand around her middle, she nodded and climbed inside the car. Until she could disarm him, she couldn't risk giving him a target. She'd protect this unexpected baby with her life and hope that when Knox realized she hadn't called him on her way to or from her appointment... he'd start searching for her.

Chapter Eleven

KNOX LEANED BACK in his chair behind his desk at the stadium and groaned, stretching sore muscles from an earlier workout. He was waiting to hear from Jade after her therapy appointment. The details were none of his business, but how she felt afterward was.

He glanced at the time on his cell and frowned. Her session was scheduled to be forty-five minutes, and he should have heard from her by now.

He patted the small box he'd slipped into his pants pocket this morning. Though he didn't plan on asking Jade to marry him today, he figured he'd keep the ring close, just in case the right moment presented itself.

He jiggled the mouse on his computer and his emails settled on the screen, but he couldn't concentrate. He tried to call Jade but it went to voicemail. He'd give her some more time and then he'd check with her office. If she wasn't at work, he'd start to worry.

Who was he kidding? He was already worried something had come up in her session that had sent her running. He drummed his fingers on the desk when he heard loud voices outside his office.

"I'm sorry but you can't just go in there." Olga sounded loud as she objected.

Knox rose just as his door flung open and Celia rushed inside. Just what he didn't need. His ex-wife giving him grief.

"I'm sorry. She pushed past me," Olga said from behind Celia.

"It's okay. I'll handle it." He nodded and Olga stepped out again.

Knox ran a hand through his hair. "Come on, Celia, I thought you had more pride than this?" She hadn't come crawling back after she'd cheated. Her pushing him now didn't make sense.

"I do. I... Look, I'm here because of Theo. He's out of control."

Knox narrowed his gaze. "I didn't know you and Theo were still... a thing." Not that he cared.

"We're not." She sat down in a chair, obviously out of breath. She took a moment and dropped her handbag on the floor. "If you hadn't blocked my number, I'd have explained sooner," she muttered. "Here's the thing. When Theo saw that first photo of you and Jade on social media, he was jealous. He told me he asked you to stay away from her, and you wouldn't listen."

"Why would I?" he asked. And the asshole hadn't asked, he'd ordered.

Celia waved her hand in the air. "Let me finish!" she said, her voice trembling. "Theo then asked me to try and get back together with you."

"To keep me away from Jade," Knox surmised.

She nodded. "Right. But obviously, it didn't work." When he opened his mouth to speak again, she held up her hand in a *stop* gesture.

"Let you finish. Got it." He leaned back against his desk, half sitting on the edge.

"I got the message that we're over, Knox. I did. I'd already felt bad about sleeping with Theo. I made so many mistakes when we were married, but I thought maybe enough time had passed and we could fix it. But I saw how furious you still were, and I knew I'd really ruined things for good." She paused, still drawing deep breaths.

"Are you okay?" He clenched and unclenched his hands, needing the information she had but knowing he had to let her tell the story her way.

She nodded. "I rushed over here. Anyway, as I'm sure you know, this past weekend, the Rockets lost in the playoffs, and I think Theo lost his mind. He called me the other day, rambling. He knows he's going to be traded."

"Only if another team wants him," Knox muttered.

"Right. The next day, he went to lunch with Holly and called me after. He looked at Holly's phone when she went to the ladies' room."

"What?" Knox was going to kill his brother. He'd known Theo was using Holly for a reason. No wonder she'd been moping around, unwilling to discuss what was wrong.

Celia tucked a strand of hair behind her ear. "He knows Jade is pregnant."

"Shit." Pacing, he paused and rubbed his eyes with his palms. "What else? Tell me quickly, because I should have heard from Jade by now and I haven't."

Celia's blue eyes opened wide. "Theo got drunk last night and called me first thing this morning. He was hungover but he had a plan. He thinks if he can get Jade somewhere alone, he can convince her to come back to him. Then he can take her away from you. He's even willing to raise your kid. He called it the ultimate fuck you."

Fury rushed through Knox. He couldn't believe Theo's arrogance. the guy was delusional. And somehow Knox had missed the signs he'd passed his normal state of arrogant behavior and had fallen off the deep end. After assuring Jade she had nothing to worry about when it came to Theo. He slammed his hand down on the desk.

He hoped Jade would think and not panic. She couldn't goad Theo or piss him off, either of which would likely send him into a rage. Knox was fucking terrified for Jade and the baby she carried. He needed to punch something harder. The wall seemed like a good option, but he decided to save his hand for Theo's face.

Celia met Knox's gaze. "Theo believes Jade is somehow the key to his life working out. That if he gets her back, he'll manage to stay with the Rockets. He'll have a family. He's really out of his mind, Knox."

"He told you all of this?"

Her eyes filled with tears as she nodded. "I never would have become involved with him if I thought he'd get so out of control."

Knox ran his fingers through his hair. "At least he told you his plan and you did the right thing."

"I tried to call Jade but she hung up on me."

Shit. Did that mean Theo had already gotten to her? Knox's stomach twisted painfully. "What else did Theo say?" he asked Celia. "Think. Did he mention where he wanted to take her?"

Celia swallowed hard. "He read Jade's messages to Holly and knew she had an early appointment this morning. When I spoke to him, he was on his way to her apartment to wait for her to come outside. I tried to call you, but you'd blocked my number. All I know is, he said he was going to take her somewhere they could be alone. That's all I know. I swear."

"Why didn't you call the police when you couldn't reach me?" he asked.

She looked away. "Theo has enough problems. I thought... I don't know what I thought, okay? But I'm here now."

He scowled at her. Hands shaking, Knox pulled out his phone and looked up Asher's number, then tapped the screen. He put the phone to his ear and waited for Jade's brother to answer.

"Hey. What's up?" Asher asked.

"Have you heard from Jade this morning?"

"No, but she had her therapy appointment," Asher said.

"Then we have a problem. I think Theo has her."

Asher let out a curse. "What the fuck? How? Why?"

"Later, okay? I'll call the cops and—"

"No," Asher bit out. "Zach is a computer genius and has connections. He knows how to find people. He'll get to her faster than bringing in the police, who'll waste time asking questions."

Knox swallowed hard, trusting Jade's brother. "Fine. Call Zach and you two get over to the stadium. Now." He disconnected the call and turned to Celia, who'd grown pale. "Do me a favor? Just sit there and think. Maybe Theo said something else that'll give us a clue as to where he's taken her."

She nodded.

Knox walked to the door, opened it, and stuck his head out. "Olga, get Holly in here, please?" Maybe his sister would have some idea where Theo would take Jade.

A few seconds later, Olga stepped inside. "Your sister is meeting with advertisers and is expected in later."

Shit. "Thanks, Olga. Make sure you leave a message for her. I need to talk to her as soon as she gets here. It's an emergency."

Knox pulled up Holly's number on his cell and tapped the screen. He listened but it went straight to voicemail and he left a message instructing her to call him back as soon as possible. Knox began pacing again as they waited for Jade's brothers or Holly to arrive. He used the time to text Asher and fill him in so they wouldn't waste precious minutes when they got here.

They sat in silence. Knox had nothing to say to his ex, though he appreciated the fact that she'd come to help. Without her, he might not have known what had happened to Jade.

Finally, Holly walked into Knox's office. She looked from Knox to Celia and her mouth opened wide.

"Don't ask. I just need to know if you have any idea where Theo might take Jade."

"What do you mean?" Holly lowered herself into the seat next to Celia. Neither said anything to each other.

Knox picked up a pen and began rolling it between his palms.

"Think of a place he liked to go when he was growing up, somewhere he mentioned often," Zach answered, entering with Asher behind him. He had a laptop in hand and walked over to where Knox sat.

Zach stared, brows raised, until Knox got the message and vacated the chair. Zach slipped off his ever-present leather jacket and settled himself behind the desk.

Opening his laptop, he powered it on while staring at Holly. "Anything come to mind?"

She rubbed her hands on her pants. "Umm…"

"Did you track her phone?" Zach asked when Holly came up blank.

At Knox's head shake, Zach began typing, doing his thing. "Asher, call Jade's doorman. Ask him if he saw her leave and, if so, what direction she went."

While Asher did as instructed, Holly tipped her head back in the chair and groaned. "I'm sorry," she mouthed to Knox. "I'm trying."

He put a hand on her shoulder. "I know. Relax and do the best you can."

"Her phone's in Yonkers. Unmoving on the Taconic. Theo must have tossed it out of the car, so we have a start on direction."

"Oh!" Holly jumped up from her seat. "When we were younger, my father owned a cabin upstate! He'd take me and Theo there, and we'd go fishing and hiking. Mom never came because she didn't like the outdoors. It wasn't one of my favorite things, either, because it had an outhouse, not a bathroom." She wrinkled her nose. "Dad left it to Theo. It was the only thing of value he had. I didn't care and never asked Theo what he did with it."

Zach's fingers flew faster on the keyboard. "Theodore Matthews… county?" he asked.

"I think Putnam," Holly said.

"According to the doorman, she walked out and headed north," Asher said, shoving his phone into his back pants pocket. "Doorman didn't see her talking to anyone."

Zach continued to type.

"What's he doing?" Holly asked.

"Probably cross-referencing Theo's name with properties owned, looking for tax information," Knox said.

"Hacking," Asher stated. "Come on, come on."

He stalked behind the desk and stood behind Zach, staring over his shoulder.

Zach ignored him.

"Got it. Sending directions to your cell, Ash." Zach hit another button on the keyboard and flipped the lid closed. "Let's hit the road."

Knox walked over to his sister. He put a hand on Holly's shoulder. "Try not to panic. Wait here and I'll let you know as soon as we've got her."

He glanced at Celia, who still sat in silence, guilt all over her face. "Stay with her," he told Holly, nodding toward his ex. He leaned close to Holly. "Be decent. Without her, we wouldn't know about any of this." He kissed her cheek and walked out behind Asher and Zach.

If his son-of-a-bitch half brother had laid a hand on Jade, Knox could guarantee Theo wouldn't be walking out of that cabin in one piece.

★　★　★

JADE SAT ON an old bed in a smelly, secluded mountain cabin with no air-conditioning. Theo looked nothing like the man she'd been engaged to—a handsome, clean-shaven playboy with a twinkle in his eye and a perpetual grin on his lips. The guy in front of her wore wrinkled clothing, had shadows beneath his eyes, and his eyes were darting all over the room, as if someone would jump out at him any second. He clearly needed help.

She mentally went through her options. If she tried to reason with him by reminding him he'd cheated on her and she was now in love with Knox and carrying his baby, she could set off his temper. Given her present condition, she didn't want to test that possibility.

She could pretend to go along with whatever he wanted, hoping he'd eventually drive them back to the city, except she couldn't bring herself to kiss him or, God forbid, do more, in an attempt to convince him he'd won against Knox.

And she'd already decided running was out of the question. Not with that knife he kept in a sheath on his belt and the gun in his hand.

She was scared but not panicked. She'd come to the realization he wouldn't hurt her if she didn't argue or fight with him. At least, not right now. How desperate he'd get, though? That was anyone's guess. He'd been muttering about losing everything and her being the key to fix his problems.

Theo had tossed her phone out the window on the way upstate. She just hoped Knox had realized she was missing and had called in the cavalry. She'd hate to think she was really on her own.

"Theo?"

He stopped his pacing.

"Did you stock this place with food? I didn't eat breakfast, and I'm hungry," she lied. She was too nauseous and nervous to eat.

The car ride had been long, and she'd already had to make do with an outhouse while Theo waited on the other side of the door. Her morning sickness had also returned in full force on the way upstate, and he'd had to pull over so she could throw up. Unfortunately, she hadn't been lucky enough for the police to stop and see if they were okay.

"Shit," he said. "I didn't plan well, but we can get you something to eat at a diner a few miles away… if we get somewhere in our talk."

She nodded, eager to get to civilization, where she could catch someone's eye and hopefully get some help. They'd been at the cabin for about an hour. During which time Theo had done more pacing than talking.

If she wanted out of here, she needed to engage him in conversation. "I'm sorry about the playoffs," she said.

He spun to face her. "If I hadn't been sitting out another suspension, we'd never have lost. They needed me. Why don't they understand how valuable I am to the team?"

She decided not to remind him of his second illegal

hit—not long after he'd served his suspension. "I know. Maybe you can sit down with your coach and explain things to him?"

He shook his head. "Coach doesn't want to hear anything I have to say." Theo began waving the gun around as he spoke, his anger and frustration making him even more irrational.

She bent her knees and pushed herself into the corner of the bed, wrapping her arms around her legs to protect her stomach—in case he fired by accident. She didn't know much about guns, and she had no idea whether or not the weapon had a safety on it.

"What do you want from me?" she asked, hoping to calm him down by changing the subject.

He spun around and walked toward her, gun pointed down. "Things were better when we were together. My career was going great, and we were happy."

She swallowed back a retort about the *great* career. Since being traded to New York, he'd been warned numerous times about his behavior—some of those warnings coming even before he'd stepped foot on the ice.

But they *had* had some happy times. Otherwise, she'd never have agreed to marry him.

"We were happy," she murmured. Until he'd cheated on her, but again, that wasn't something she'd bring up now.

"See?" He sat down on the mattress, too close for comfort. "We *can* be that way again. I'm even willing to raise Knox's spawn as my own." He chuckled at the idea and her stomach rolled over.

He'd crossed the boundary of sane. He was alternately deluding himself that they could be a happy couple and delighting in the notion of taking something from Knox. And Jade and the peanut in her belly were stuck smack in the middle.

And if his mental instability wasn't bad enough, Theo reeked of booze. She had no doubt he'd been drunk last night and hadn't showered before executing this brilliant plan. The trip upstate had been hell. Between concern for her baby, herself and what he'd do to her once they arrived at this cabin, she'd driven herself to panic. Not to mention the utter fear of him driving drunk. Once at the cabin, she had to deal with the smells of this musty, dusty room, and Theo's body odor—all things that could trigger a migraine. That was the last thing she needed. If she was going to get out of this, she needed to be clear headed.

She also needed space from him, both for her physical and mental well-being.

She inhaled, trying to calm her racing pulse, but gagged from the smell.

"Are you going to be sick again?" he asked in disgust.

She shrugged. "I don't know. Some bottled water would help. I thought I saw one in the car?"

He eyed her warily. "I'll be right back." He rose and waved the gun at her, causing her to duck in fear. "Don't move from this spot. I'll hear you if you try and run."

She believed him.

Even though this place was in the middle of nowhere, Theo had hidden the vehicle in the back of the house. He walked out of the cabin, and she heard him stomping around outside. She blew out a long breath and leaned against the wall, desperately trying to come up with a plan of escape.

Knox's nerves were strung tight as they pulled off the highway and drove the couple of miles off the beaten path, following the directions Zach had sent to Asher's cell. He had no way of knowing Theo's state of mind or what his brother was capable of if cornered.

Zach, who'd been driving, stopped at the edge of a dirt road and put the GMC Sierra truck in park.

"Why stop here?" Asher asked before Knox could.

"We don't want Theo to hear us coming. So we're walking the last half mile."

Then Zach led the way, and Asher and Knox followed.

"Should we call the police?" Asher asked.

"I already have cop friends searching the city. Right now, all we have is a hunch that she's here. It's not a real lead. I'm sure the three of us can handle Theo if he's here. I assume I'm the only one packing?" Zach patted his jacket.

Maybe that explained why he never took the damned thing off. "Yes," Asher said, the word sounding more like *duh*, shooting Knox an eye roll as they walked.

"Maybe I can talk him down." Knox didn't want anything to happen to his stepbrother—beyond getting his ass put in prison for kidnapping, that is.

Zach stopped short. "There." He pointed to what looked like a log cabin. The shades were drawn and it looked deserted. "I'm going to do a quick check. Stay here and we'll regroup after my recon." He walked off, taking the woods as an indirect route.

Knox turned to Asher. "Who *is* he?" he asked.

Asher shrugged. "Bar owner slash something he's never admitted. We just know we can come to him for anything." He glanced at the cabin, his eyes full of concern. "Tell me Theo won't hurt her."

"I'm counting on it." Knox's hands curled into fists. "His main goal in life is to get something over on me. If he can win Jade back—or just think he has—he wins. As long as Jade doesn't provoke him, she's okay." At least, that was what he needed to believe.

Knox caught a glimpse of Zach casing the house, checking windows before he disappeared around the side. His heart pounded in his chest as he waited for confirmation that Jade was in there. He needed to be doing something, not standing here twiddling his thumbs.

They waited in silence, sweat dripping down Knox's face until Zach returned, popping up from the other side of the woods. "Theo's car's parked out back. They're both inside."

"Thank God." Knox blew out a breath.

"Okay, what next?" Asher asked.

Before Zach could reply, the cabin door opened and Theo stepped outside. He glanced around and Knox held his breath. But thanks to Zach, they were well hidden in the trees. Theo shut the front door and headed around back.

"Okay, boys, that's our cue." Neither Knox nor Asher could compare to Zach when it came to stealth, but they made it to the cabin and walked inside without issue.

Jade sat huddled in the corner of a bed, and her eyes opened wide at the sight of them. Zach put his finger to his lips and she nodded.

Knox rushed over and she flew into his arms. He held her tight, her legs wrapped around his waist, her arms around his neck.

Zach stood beside the front door, waiting for Theo, with Asher behind him, ready to help if needed.

"I found it," Theo said, stepping inside, a water bottle in his hand.

Zach cold-cocked him with his handgun, and Theo crumpled to the floor. "Oops." He grinned as he pulled handcuffs from inside his jacket and cuffed Theo's wrists behind him. "You okay, sis?"

"Yeah." She gripped Knox's neck, holding on for dear life.

"You're safe," Knox whispered in her ear.

Still clinging to him, she turned and took in the sight of Theo passed out on the floor. "Jesus. Is he alive?"

Asher scowled. "I care more that *you're* alive."

"How did you find me?" she asked.

Knox was happy she held on to him and breathed in the coconut scent of her shampoo. Having her in his arms calmed him down.

"A combination of Celia doing the right thing, Zach tracking your phone, and its location triggering Holly's memory of the cabin," Asher explained.

"Celia! She called me this morning and told me not to go anywhere with Theo. But he came up behind me and took me by surprise." Jade shook her head. "I can't believe she tried to help."

"Thank God she did," Knox muttered.

Asher stepped closer. "Can you put her down so I can see for myself that my sister's okay?"

Knox growled but let Jade slide down his body. He felt every inch of her, reassuring himself she was fine.

She hugged her brothers and thanked them for finding her when a low moan sounded from the floor.

"What happened?" Theo asked, his voice groggy. He struggled and realized he was confined. "Fuck. Who cuffed me?"

Jade walked over to the man who'd caused her so much pain. "Have you lost your mind?" she shouted at him.

"What? You said we could talk!" Theo yelled back.

"Because you threatened to hurt my baby!" Without warning, she kicked him in the ribs.

"Ouch! Dammit, cut that out. I just wanted you back."

She turned away from him and glanced at Knox. "Take me home."

Knox looked her over. Physically, she appeared fine, if tired, but he needed to be sure. "I'd rather have you checked at the hospital."

She shook her head. "He didn't hurt me. I just want to go home. I have an appointment with a doctor tomorrow, anyway."

Knox didn't like it, but he nodded.

Zach tossed Asher the keys to his truck. "You guys go. I'll call the cops and have them take out the garbage. I'm sure they'll want to talk to Jade, but I'll let them know where to find her."

"How will you get home?" Jade asked her brother.

"Don't worry about me. You need to go home and rest." He placed his hand on her stomach. "You gave us all a scare."

She smiled. "I'm fine. And if the police need anything from me, a statement or something, I'm more than ready to help." She frowned at Theo, then shook her head. "Come on." Grabbing Knox's hand, she started for the door.

He paused and looked down at his half sibling. As angry as Knox had been at Theo, he didn't recognize the pathetic man cuffed on the floor and couldn't conjure up the fury he'd felt earlier. "You could have had it all, you know. Now I just hope you get the help you need. From inside a jail cell."

Squeezing Jade's hand tight, they walked around Theo and out the front door.

KNOX INSISTED ON sitting in the back of Zach's truck cab with Jade, while Asher grumbled about feeling like a damned chauffeur. Jade laughed and snuggled into Knox's arms, giving him peace for the first time since he'd discovered she was missing.

Fifteen minutes after they'd left the cabin, the police had called Asher's phone, wanting to speak to Jade. They were annoyed she'd left the scene before they had time to get her statement. Asher told them her lawyer would be in touch, and she'd talk to them then before disconnecting the call.

Once back in the city, Asher had dropped Knox and Jade at her apartment. Knox ordered in food while she showered. Then they sat and ate deli sandwiches in silence. The ring sat in his pocket, taunting him. But he didn't think this was the right time. Not after everything Jade had been through today. He didn't want to take advantage of her vulnerability now.

She was quiet and he gave her the space she needed.

She picked up her remnants of her meal, stood, and tossed them in the trash. "Knox?" She turned toward him.

"Hmm?"

"You're very quiet. Are you upset about Theo's arrest? Worried about Holly? What is it?"

Her worry for him touched his heart, especially since he thought the silence had been her doing. "I was just wondering what was going on in your mind."

He stood and tossed out his garbage, as well. "I spoke to Holly while you were in the shower. She's okay. Miles is taking good care of her."

"That's good. And Celia? I still can't believe she was involved. Is she in trouble?" Jade asked.

"I hope not. All she did was try to get me back in her life. As soon as Theo's plan went crazy, she spoke up." He might not want to be married to Celia—and would definitely never trust her again—but he couldn't deny she had done the right thing.

Jade nodded.

"Holly said that Celia left my office once she knew we'd found you. I assume that's the last we'll hear from her."

"I can't say that's a disappointment, but I am grateful for her help." Jade yawned, covering her mouth. "Excuse me."

He walked over and cupped her face in his hands. "You have to be exhausted."

She nodded. "I am."

"I should go and let you get some rest."

She shook her head, causing him to release her face. "Don't go. I have some things I want to talk to you about." She clasped his hand. "Come on. Let's relax."

She led him into her bedroom and the heaviness in his chest eased. Though he didn't know what was going through her mind, the fact that she wanted him here was enough. She stretched out on the bed, patting the mattress beside her. He walked around to the other side and settled in.

She turned to face him and he did the same.

"Did I tell you I made Theo stop so I could throw up on the side of the road?" she asked.

He laughed. "You sound awfully pleased with yourself."

"I am. At least I made him suffer some."

"You gave him a good kick, too."

Her eyes sparkled with mirth. "He deserved it." She sat up and curled her legs beneath him, facing him.

He pushed himself up against the headboard, ready to hear whatever she had to say. He studied her face. Though pale, even without makeup, she was beautiful.

"So I had a lot of time to think as we drove up to the cabin." She rubbed her arms with her hands. "I knew I couldn't run because Theo had a gun and he'd made it clear he'd shoot. He had a knife, too. But as long as I was calm, I wasn't too worried that he would hurt me. So I stopped panicking and started thinking about you."

"I'm sorry you got caught in whatever the hell this thing is between me and Theo." He tucked her hair behind her ear. "I was worried when I didn't hear from you and then terrified when Celia told me what he planned."

"It's not your fault." Jade gave him a small smile, one he appreciated. "Now to the important things."

"I'm listening."

She nodded and drew a deep breath, her fingers plucking at the comforter on the bed. "When you and I met up again, I had more walls built around my heart than a castle. But each time we were together, those walls came down, one by one, starting with that first kiss."

He grinned. "It wasn't just a simple kiss, was it?" He skimmed his knuckles over her cheek.

She shook her head. "No. It bound us. More and more, you let me see who you are inside." She touched his shirt over his heart. "You're such a good man. And I kept asking myself whether or not I could believe in what I saw."

She looked him in the eye, her face full of an emotion he didn't dare name. "You made it impossible for me not to fall in love with you. I knew it on the island but was too afraid to say it out loud. Then Theo pulled a gun, and the whole ride to the cabin, I thought, what if I waited too long? What if I'd never be able to tell Knox how I felt about him?"

His heart slowed as he waited. Reaching out, he stroked her cheek. "Say it now."

Her smile grew wide. "I love you, Knox Sinclair."

His heart began to beat faster as she said the words that made everything right in his world. "And I love you, Jade Dare."

Her sparkling eyes and wide grin lit him up inside, and he decided it was time, feeling more certain of her answer now than when he'd initially purchased the ring.

She leaned forward and her lips met his. Their connection went soul deep, because they were finally on the same page. In no rush, he kissed her for a long time, their tongues twining, their lips locked.

Finally, he was ready. He broke the kiss, then grinned before rolling off his side of the bed to stand. Reaching into his pocket, he pulled out the box that had been poking at him all day—a reminder that they had a future once she was back home with him. He walked around to her side of the mattress.

"What are you doing?" She wrinkled her nose in confusion.

He dropped to one knee. "Jade, there is nothing I want more than to spend the rest of my life with you. And before you say anything, I want you to know that I would have asked you to marry me even if you weren't pregnant with my baby. That's a bonus for us both. But I love you more than life itself. Will you marry me?" He lifted the top of the box.

Her eyes opened wide, her gaze on his and not the ring. As much as he appreciated her lack of materialism, he really wanted to see her reaction.

"How? When did you go shopping?" she asked.

"I took Asher with me earlier in the week. Now will you please answer me? And look at the ring?"

Keeping her gaze steady on his, she said, "Yes. I will marry you." Then she glanced down and squealed in excitement as she looked at the ring he'd picked out just for her.

"It's a heart… I love it."

He stood and pulled the ring out of the box, then slid it over her finger. "I picked a heart because you own mine."

"It fits," she said, wriggling her fingers.

"Thank Lauren."

Laughing, she wrapped her arms around his neck and buried her face in his neck. "This is one wedding I promise will go off without a hitch."

"Damn right." He lifted her so he could sit, then settled her on his lap. "I'd planned to pop the question after your doctor's appointment tomorrow, but something made me grab the ring and keep it with me today."

"Intuition," she murmured. "I'm glad we're here and alone when you did."

He thought about the type of affair they might

have. "Are you set on the idea of a big wedding?" he asked.

"God no. After all I've been through? I just want to say I do," she said.

He toyed with a long strand of her hair, happier than he could ever remember being. "Good." He didn't want a spectacle, though he'd give her anything she desired. "I'd like to do it before the baby is born if that's okay with you."

"Yes." She threaded her fingers through his hair as they talked. "And while we're at it, I'd like to get married before I start showing."

He placed his hand over her flat belly, excited to see her grow bigger with his child. "I'm sure you and Serenity will get started planning soon."

Anticipation lit up her expression. "Speaking of relatives, you have a choice."

He raised an eyebrow. "What's that?"

"We can make phone calls now, telling our families the good news…" Her voice trailed off.

"Or?"

"We can do this." She straddled his lap and pushed him back onto the mattress. "Take just one more night for ourselves before we spread the news."

He pulled her down until their lips met in a kiss, giving her his answer. Not only would she always come first with him but kissing her would always be his favorite pastime.

Epilogue

One month later

JADE AND HER siblings gathered for the day in their parents' lush backyard by the pool. She stretched out and relaxed under an umbrella, with only her legs in the sun. Her wedding was in one week, and she couldn't wait to marry Knox right here, surrounded by the people she loved.

During the last four weeks, she'd started the therapy she'd missed, courtesy of Theo. Had she come to terms with what Audrey had done? Not yet. Was she still angry? She'd like to think her heart was too full for negative emotion, but there was a tiny corner that still hurt.

As for Theo, he was no longer an issue. Jade had given her statement to the police, and Theo had agreed to a plea deal in exchange for a sentence in a mental facility. The prosecutor, Assistant District Attorney Scarlett Grayson, had asked Jade if she was okay with the potential sentence. For Holly's sake, and the Theo she once knew, she'd agreed. Jade had liked Scarlett and how concerned she was about victim's rights.

Holly was sad but adjusting, and Jade had brought her into the Dare family. She and Miles were here, enjoying the bright summer day and healing from the pain her brother had caused.

Beside her, Knox and Asher stood talking, looking at something on their cell phone screen.

She stood and joined them. "Hi, guys."

"What's up? You two looked deep in conversation."

Asher slipped his cell into the pocket of his board shorts.

"You know our friend Derek Bettencourt?" he asked.

She nodded. "Business school buddy. He was on your Vegas trip, right?"

"That's him," Knox said.

"Isn't he Senator Bettencourt's son?" Aurora had walked over to join them. She was also in a one-piece bathing suit, and her cute baby bump was visible.

"The senator is also a presidential nominee," Knox said. "And yes, Derek is his son."

"He's a fly under the radar kind of guy. The senator's daughter, on the other hand, can't seem to stay out of the headlines," Asher muttered, a frown on his face.

His opinion of Derek's sister was definitely not good, Jade thought.

"What's her name?" Aurora asked. "Bettencourt sounds familiar to me, and not because of politics."

"Nicolette Bettencourt."

Aurora's eyes widened with recognition. "I follow her on social media. She's a model and an influencer." Aurora waved at Nick, who was approaching with Leah's hand in his. The imp had red ice pop stain all over her face, and it wasn't even lunchtime yet.

Aurora shook her head and sighed. "I need to make sure he's not spoiling her rotten. I'll be back."

Jade laughed and rubbed her own belly, wondering if she was having a boy or a girl. She and Knox hadn't yet decided if they wanted to know in advance. Knox's hand covered her own as they cradled her stomach.

"Nicolette is trouble," Asher was saying.

Jade narrowed her gaze. "That's harsh. I hope you don't tell Derek your feelings about his sister. And it's a good thing you don't have to spend any time with her. Something tells me you wouldn't be able to hide your feelings."

Asher frowned. "Of course I wouldn't say anything to Derek. But she has a public reputation. It's not like I'm making things up."

Jade settled her hands on her hips, not happy with her brother's stubbornness and judgmental attitude. "She's only twenty-one years old. Barely an adult. I think pegging her as trouble isn't fair."

Knox squeezed her tighter, a warning for her to relax. She understood he was worried about her anxiety and the baby's health but Jade knew she was fine.

"Then I guess we'll have to agree to disagree," Asher said. "But one thing is certain. Today's photos are going to hurt her father's reputation."

At that statement, Knox muttered in agreement.

"What photos?" Jade asked.

"Someone sold compromising pictures of her and posted them online," Knox said.

"Naked ones?" Jade asked, horrified. "That poor girl."

"What was she doing putting herself in a position for the photos to be taken in the first place?" Asher asked.

Jade glared at her oldest brother. "Oh, I don't know. Are you saying *you* didn't do stupid things when you were young?"

"He was born old," Layla said, laughing as she walked by.

Their younger sister had friends coming over today and was lost in her teenage world as she headed to her room.

"Kid's got a point about you." Knox raised an eyebrow and glanced at Asher, laughing before turning to Jade. "Do you want a bottle of cold water?"

She nodded. "I'll come with you. Asher, want anything?"

His cell rang, interrupting them before he could answer. He glanced at the screen. "It's Derek." He held up a finger for them to wait before answering the call. "Hey. You okay?"

Asher might be judgmental and uptight, but he worried about his family and close friends.

"Sure. Of course I'll be there. See you soon," Asher said.

"What's going on?" Knox asked, slipping his hand into Jade's.

She appreciated the warmth and security she'd found with him and promised herself that she'd never take it—or him—for granted.

Asher raised his shoulders. "I don't know. Derek wants to talk about her going to the island until the news cycle blows over. But he wants to discuss it in person."

"What could he want that he can't ask over the phone?" Jade wondered aloud.

"Not a clue."

"Well, good luck," Jade said. "Will you come back here later?"

"I'll try." Asher snagged his shirt from a lounge chair and walked over to their parents to say goodbye.

Jade turned to Knox and slid her hands around his

waist. "Any idea what Derek wants from him?" she asked.

Knox shook his head. "But Derek has a big closing this week. If he wants to send Nicolette to the island, he can't go with her."

"Maybe he'll ask Asher to take her instead," Jade said with a grin.

Knox rolled his eyes. "You'd like that, wouldn't you, my little troublemaker." He reached around to playfully pinch her ass and she squealed.

"Cut that out," she muttered, but she didn't mind one bit.

Lifting on her toes, she pressed her lips to his. "One month," she reminded him.

Knox treated her to the sexy grin she loved so much. "I can't wait for you to become Mrs. Sinclair. Actually, I can't wait to make love to you *after* you're Mrs. Sinclair."

She shook her head. "Really? That's caveman behavior. Next thing I know, you'll be banging your chest and declaring that I'm *your woman*." She was giving him a hard time but it was more on principle. Jade was happy to take his name, and if it turned him on for her to be *Mrs. Sinclair*, she knew the pleasure would be all hers.

Without warning, he swung her into his arms.

"What are you doing?" she squealed, wrapping her

arms around his neck. She hung on as he walked past her entire family, who'd decided to clap as they passed. Her cheeks heated at being the center of attention.

"I'm taking you somewhere private so I can remind you of all the good reasons you *want* to be *my woman*—caveman behavior or not."

"Don't forget, it goes both ways." She rested her chin on his shoulder and nipped at his ear. "But put me down. I'm not having sex in my parents' house."

He shook his head and touched his forehead to hers. "Next thing I know you'll tell me no sleeping together until the wedding."

"Hmm. Now that's an interesting idea. It could make the wedding night that much better. All the anticipation..." She wriggled seductively against him and his cock thickened, hating the idea he'd said in jest.

He groaned and let her slide down so her feet touched the floor, her body gliding against his. "God, no."

She pressed her lips to his. "Don't worry. I can't resist you any more than you can resist me."

And he knew she'd never run from him again, in any way.

He blew out an obviously relieved breath. "Damn straight. You're mine, Jade Dare. Always."

"I absolutely am. And you, Knox Sinclair, are everything I ever wanted. Now let's go enjoy the bright summer day and celebrate our equally bright future."

He grasped her around the waist and kissed her until someone let out a catcall, and they stepped apart, laughing. He was everything she'd ever wanted, too, and she'd never let him forget it.

Thanks for reading! Asher Dare is next! Find out how he handles his best friend's sexy, younger sister in JUST ONE TASTE!

Keep turning for a sneak peek!

JUST ONE TASTE EXCERPT

Note: This is an early version of Chapter One. Names and things subject to change! Enjoy!

NICOLETTE BETTENCOURT WOKE up and reached for her cell phone. The ringer and notifications had been on silent all night, and she checked her email and texts first thing in the morning. Upon turning on her phone, she couldn't keep up with the messages and notifications popping up.

She pushed herself to a sitting position and focused on a message from her modeling agent, Amelia Mitchell: *Open this and call me immediately. You're all over the internet.*

She looked at the link to the biggest online tabloid, known for breaking stories in celebrity and entertainment news, and her stomach pitched. Whatever it was, it couldn't be good.

She clicked and studied the photo on the screen, trying to process what she saw. It was her bedroom, with the familiar chandelier hanging from the ceiling, the twin floral framed photos on the wall above the headboard, and the domed smart light on the right nightstand because Nikki found it difficult to wake up on workdays. *What the hell?*

Her pale pink duvet lay rumpled on one side of the bed, and the part she'd avoided looking at until now, the female lying asleep on the other side. Nikki tried but found it impossible to swallow. Heart pounding, she enlarged the picture, even though she already knew. *She* was the girl lying naked in bed, her ass exposed for the world to see. *But how?*

Nauseous now, she scrolled lower only to find another photo of herself, her hair pulled up into a messy bun, her face visible as she slept on her back. Censorship bars covered her private parts, but she was naked nonetheless. Shame washed over her and she started to tremble.

How did someone take photos of me in my own home? Tears filled her eyes and she glanced down at her *nude* body—because that's how she slept—and freaked out. She jumped out of bed, grabbed the silk robe slung over the footboard, and wrapped the material around herself, shaking as she tied the sash tight around her waist.

She felt exposed, violated, and utterly petrified.

Nikki wasn't ready to talk to her manager or anyone else, for that matter. She scrolled through her phone, seeing her mother had called no less than a dozen times. Her parents would be furious, worried about how this would impact her senator father's presidential campaign.

Any other twenty-one-year-old girl would call a friend, but Nikki didn't have anyone she trusted completely. Not even Meg Cologne, another model she was closest to. But that wasn't saying much about their friendship. Meg wasn't the warm-fuzzy type, and Nikki needed someone to comfort her, not gloat. And Meg was the gloating type.

Her doorbell rang and she froze. She couldn't face anyone. Not now. Then she remembered the doorman would only let a select few people come up without calling. People she could handle seeing.

Pulling her robe tighter, she walked into the main area of her apartment and tiptoed to the door.

Someone banged again and rang the bell. "Come on, Nikki. Let me in."

She let out a breath of relief and opened the door. "Derek!" She fell into her big brother's arms, not bothering to hold back choking sobs.

"Come on." He wrapped an arm around her and walked them inside, shutting the door and locking it behind them. "I don't have to ask if you're okay, but how did this happen? How were pictures like that taken and exposed?"

She pushed herself out of his embrace. "I don't know, okay? I admit I sleep naked but nobody's been here!"

"No guys? Boyfriends or otherwise?" he asked.

She shook her head. "Not since Lance last year. I'll be right back." She rushed to the bathroom and grabbed some tissues, blotting her eyes and wetting her face before rejoining her brother in the family room.

"Have you spoken to Lance lately?"

"No. We broke up last year, and it was fairly amicable as those things go." She lifted her shoulders. "That was it. I swear to you I have no idea how anyone got in here while I was sleeping. And that had to be what happened, right?" She shivered at the possibility.

Derek's scowl would scare anyone except her. Nikki knew he wasn't angry at her, he was pissed and worried. "I'll figure that part out."

Her phone rang from the bedroom and she groaned. "Mom's been calling nonstop. So has my agent. I didn't look to see who else left messages. I just know I've been slammed with notifications, too. I don't want to know." She grew queasy at the thought of anyone viewing those photos, yet she knew half the world had seen them by now. Senator Corbin Bettencourt's daughter was in the headlines again.

Derek put a calming hand on her shoulder. "Go get your phone and call Mom while I'm here. Then we'll figure out our next move."

Knowing he was right, she nodded. She walked to

her room and picked up her phone, suddenly uncomfortable being in the bedroom that had always been her comfort space.

She returned to Derek, who'd taken or made a phone call of his own.

Her cell rang again and *Mom* showed up on the screen. "Might as well get it over with," she muttered. Drawing a deep breath, she took the call. "Hello?"

"Nicolette Anne," her mother cried out, her voice shrill, as she used Nikki's longer, proper name her parents preferred, refusing to call her Nikki, the nickname *she'd* chosen. "How could you let such a thing happen! Do you have any idea how mortifying this is for your father?"

What about what how awful it is for me, Nikki wondered, not voicing the thought out loud. Her mother wouldn't care. Thank God she had Derek by her side and always had.

Seeing he'd put a hand to his ear to block her voice, she took a few steps away so they could each hear their respective callers.

"It's not like I posed for the photo, Mother. Someone somehow took pictures of me when I was sleeping. They violated my privacy!"

"Come now. Do you really think I believe such a thing? You've constantly disappointed us. Between your grades in school and the issues with being on time for modeling shoots, your name in the papers when your contract details leaked—"

Nikki blinked, hating the tears her mother managed to bring out so easily. Normally she tried to be immune to the *you're a disappointment* theme, but she was in a vulnerable place, and her mother was using it against her.

"There were legitimate reasons for those things, too," Nikki reminded her mother.

Heaven forbid Collette Bettencourt acknowledged her daughter's issues. She'd inherited dyslexia from her mother's brother, and Nikki's inability to read well had resulted in poor grades in school. Her mother never allowed tutors because nobody could find out Nicolette wasn't perfect.

"Nicolette, are you listening?" her mother asked, her annoyed tone one Nikki was used to hearing.

"I'm here."

Her mother had been asking how they were going to explain naked pictures of their daughter to the press and digging in on what an embarrassment Nicolette was to the family, so Nikki had tuned her out.

"I'm not interested in anything but making this go away. Who took the pictures?" her mother asked.

"I told you, I don't know."

Derek finished his call, slipped his phone into his pants pocket, and walked over, holding out his arm, palm up.

Nikki handed him the phone. Their mother's voice sounded loud as her complaining continued. "Mother."

At the sound of Derek's voice, she stopped her berating and changed her tone. "Derek, honey, please help us. Your sister—"

"Is in trouble, or don't you care? Her privacy has been violated, she's scared to death, and all you can think about is Dad's career. If you can't find compassion for your daughter, leave her alone. Goodbye, Mother." He disconnected the call and turned to Nikki. "Now that's taken care of. Let's talk."

Nodding, she followed him into the kitchen. In a daze, she made them cups of coffee, finding the chore of doing something routine helpful to calm her nerves.

After she'd put milk and sugar on the table and joined him, they each doctored their morning brew.

Derek met her gaze. "The paparazzi are going to swarm outside the building soon, if they haven't already. I'd like to get you out of here."

Her stomach twisted at the thought. "And go where?"

Derek reached out and covered her hand with his. "I have an idea but you need to trust me. I'm going to talk to Asher," he said of his close friend.

Asher, the man she remembered as a sexy, brooding man she barely knew, but she recalled making an awful impression on him.

"Asher has an estate on Windermere Island. It's off Eleuthera, near the Bahamas. You can lie low there until something else takes over the news cycle. You'll be safe and no one will think to look for you there."

"Will you come with me?"

Derek placed his hand over hers. "I wish I could but I have a closing this week."

"Oh, right." Derek's company, Bettencourt Inc., was purchasing a start-up social media group he planned to incorporate into his media conglomerate. She didn't want to make him feel any worse, so she forced a small smile. "Okay. If you think that's best."

He nodded. "I do. If Asher is on board, I'll be back to take you to his private jet. Can you pack while I'm gone?"

She narrowed her gaze. "Are you sure you know what you're doing?"

Asher Dare was the last person she wanted to go with. He'd seen her at her worst. She'd been coming home from a rough photo shoot in Mexico. She was tired, miserable, and couldn't wait to get home when a customs agent had pulled her over thanks to a medication bottle from a Mexican pharmacy they'd found in her bag. Nobody believed she hadn't bought the drugs herself, that she'd been set up, and flashes of being arrested went through her mind during the question-ing.

By the time her pissed-off father had done his magic and gotten her out of there, she'd been sweaty, had to pee for hours, and her parents' yelling had her even more upset.

The senator had left her with Derek … and Asher. She admitted now she'd been obnoxious and rude, but after what she'd been through, it was a miracle she hadn't been a puddle on the floor. Asher's overall impression of her hadn't been a good one.

He rose and walked over, bracing an arm around her shoulder. "Do you want to stay in Manhattan until things die down and we figure out who did this?"

Her eyes filled again, the thought of being where it had happened more terrifying. "No."

He rose to his full height. "I'm going to ask Asher in person. I'll take an Uber and be back as soon as I can. Meanwhile, you're safe here. Not only did I put the fear of God into Preston at the desk downstairs but I have a bodyguard hanging around incognito on the front sidewalk and another out back. Nobody's getting into the building who doesn't belong."

They both knew her father should be the one who should hire security for his daughter. He was the parent. It wasn't Derek's responsibility, but here he was, stepping up. As always. "Love you," she said.

"Love you, too, peanut," he said, using the nickname he'd had for her as she was growing up.

She wrinkled her nose. "Don't call me that."

When she was born, he'd been twelve and an amazing big brother from day one. He reached out and tweaked her nose with his thumb and forefinger, another holdout from when she was a kid. "I'll be back. Don't let anyone in you don't know."

Nodding, she walked him to the door and locked up behind him.

ASHER LEFT A family barbecue early to meet Derek Bettencourt, a business school buddy, at Asher's office. Already aware that Derek's younger sister, Nicolette, had gotten herself into yet another situation that required fixing, Asher wondered what Derek wanted that he couldn't have asked over the phone.

Asher had met Nicolette twice. Once when she was a kid and once when she was seventeen and he'd gone with Derek to pick her up at the airport. She'd been late, and it had taken a ridiculous amount of time to find out she'd been caught by customs with illegal drugs in her bag.

She swore someone had set her up. Derek had believed her. The senator and his wife had not. Asher had been prepared to feel bad for her, but when she'd come out, she'd been a spoiled, pissy, rude brat, and like the senator, he hadn't been sure whether or not to trust her word.

Shaking his head, he pulled into the parking garage below the Dirty Dare Spirits offices in Midtown West. The company and the building were owned by Asher and his siblings but run by Asher himself. As it was a long July Fourth weekend, the building was quiet.

The interior design consisted of four bars spread out on the ground level. Each served a variety of coffee and alcohol, depending on the time of day. A separate floor held a lab where mixologists created craft cocktails, and the office space was on the floors above.

He took the elevator from the underground garage to the ground level, stepped out, and walked toward the front entrance just as Derek stepped inside the front doors.

Asher strode over, greeting him with a brotherly hug and pat on the back.

"Thanks for coming. I figured this place was the easiest for us to meet." Derek ran a hand through his already messed jet-black hair, a sure sign he had a lot on his mind.

"No problem. Let's go upstairs and talk. Want coffee?" Asher offered. The coffee bars were closed but he could make them drinks.

Derek shook his head. "I'm wired enough already. Thanks."

They started to walk toward the elevators, and Asher nodded at the weekend security guard. "Hi, Tim. Good holiday weekend with the family?"

The older man, who'd worked there prior to Asher buying the building, nodded. "We had our barbecue yesterday. Thanks for asking, Mr. Dare."

Asher smiled. "Have a good one."

He and Derek took the elevator to his office floor. Once inside, Asher turned on the light. They settled into the comfortable chairs in the corner across from his desk, and Asher waited for Derek to talk.

"You've seen the photos?" Derek finally asked.

Not wanting to make things worse, Asher said, "Just a glimpse."

"But enough to know what we're dealing with."

"Yeah. Is your father livid?" Asher said.

Derek's expression grew furious, his mouth turning downward in a scowl. "Not for the reasons he should be. As usual, he's concerned with his reputation. I'm worried about my sister. Somehow, someone got into her apartment to take those photographs and she's a mess. Scared, embarrassed, you name it. I'm not sure there are enough words to cover it."

Asher winced. Jade was right. He'd been judgmental without knowing the facts. Still, once again,

Nicolette was in trouble that she claimed someone else had caused.

"What can I do?" Asher still couldn't imagine why Derek had requested they meet.

"I know this is a big ask, but I need to get Nikki out of town until things blow over in the press. It'll also give me time to have someone figure out when and how those photos were taken."

Asher met his friend's gaze. "You want her to go to the island? No problem." Once Dirty Dare Vodka, as it was then known, had succeeded, he'd bought his getaway that had become a family escape.

Derek steepled his fingers, his gaze steady on Asher's. "I want you to go with her to the island and stay so she's not alone."

Asher blinked in shock. "Seriously? Why don't *you* take her? I'm sure she'd be more comfortable with her brother than someone she barely knows."

Inclining his head, Derek groaned. "You're right and I would, but I have a deal closing this week."

"Shit. Does she want to go with a friend?" Asher wouldn't mind letting two women use the guest rooms at his house. That way he could do his friend a favor and avoid babysitting someone with a penchant for finding trouble.

Derek shook his head. "Our family name makes it hard for her to trust people. People in the modeling industry think she got where she is because of her family connections. There have been a number of incidents in social media and the news that make her look bad."

Of course there have.

Derek leaned forward. "Listen, I wouldn't ask if I didn't really need the favor. I can't send her alone, she's too shaken up, and I *trust* you."

Asher pinched the bridge of his nose. He didn't have any pressing business coming up, but he wouldn't be the best company for a young woman with whom he had nothing in common. One he wasn't sure was as innocent as her brother believed. Not the way she jet-set across the world modeling and with the fast crowd he'd seen photos of her running with.

"I didn't want to do this," Derek said in the wake of Asher's silence. "But remember the stage-five clinger you couldn't shake? *You owe me.*"

Asher groaned. That woman had been impossible to dump. He'd tried being pleasant but she wouldn't take a hint. She'd brought him lunch every day at work for a week until he'd had to tell the guard to turn her away. She'd shown up outside his apartment every time he went to the gym, and he'd had to change his schedule. He had no idea how she'd known where he lived or what his plans were until he'd discovered she'd befriended his personal assistant, who shared his information. Then he'd had two women to get rid of.

Asher had been at his favorite upscale bar with Derek, and she'd shown up without being invited. Apparently she'd decided the best way to get Asher's attention was to make him jealous, and she started hanging all over Derek.

"She sure as fuck transferred her affections easily enough, and then she became *my* problem. I had to change my cell phone number and make out a police report," Derek muttered.

The man had a point. Asher did owe him. Besides, he'd been about to agree anyway. "Okay. I was just wrapping my head around the idea of taking Nicolette to the island."

"She likes to be called Nikki. Only my parents call her Nicolette."

"And the media," Asher muttered, but once they reached the hangar, they wouldn't have to worry about the paps.

"Thank you." Derek slapped him on the back. "Because there are only a handful of friends I trust with my baby sister, and you're one of them. Plus you have a house on an island," he said with a chuckle. "Look at it this way. This time I owe *you* one."

"It's no problem," Asher lied, but he'd do anything for his friend, and not because of the stage-five clinger.

"I'll bring Nikki to Teterboro," Derek said of the private airport where Asher kept his jet.

Asher nodded, wondering how the hell he'd handle being alone with a twenty-one-year-old girl with a diva-like reputation who'd no doubt been spoiled throughout her life. Even if it seemed to be a way for her parents to keep her at arm's length. Knowing what it was like to have a close family, he felt a tug of conscience for what she'd been through, but at least she'd had her brother.

Asher would give anything for Derek to have chosen anyone else for this job, but as he'd pointed out, Asher had the home on the island. And a promise was a promise. Even if this trip was guaranteed to be the longest of his life.

WHILE NIKKI PACKED for the beach and hiding out, her cell phone rang. Wary, she glanced at the screen, seeing Meg's name flash on the screen.

She answered on the second ring. "Hi, Meg."

"Girl, what is going on with you?" Megan Cologne, a name she'd chosen for her career, yelled into the phone. "The whole world has seen your ass."

Nikki winced. Though Meg could be crass and blunt, she was the only one nice to Nikki when they were surrounded by other models. The rest had labeled her a diva, and her life on the runway was basically a version of *Mean Girls*. More and more, Nikki wanted out of the life she hadn't really chosen, but now wasn't the time to think that far into the future.

"Can you not remind me about what the world has seen?" Disturbed, she looked around her bedroom and pulled down the shade even though she wasn't facing another window and nobody could see into her bedroom.

"Don't worry about anything. Knowing you, you'll make lemonade out of this mess."

Nikki rolled her eyes and packed a few more bathing suits. "You seem to think my life is charmed. I can assure you it's not."

Meg snorted and Nikki ignored the comment, discussing the mean comments on the sites showing the photos, all the while assuring Nikki things would pass. The beautiful blonde had grown up poor and arrived in Manhattan with nothing more than a backpack and a dream of being a model. Nikki considered Meg lucky she hadn't met the wrong person before finding a job at an independent clothing store whose owner had friends in the right places.

A knock sounded on her door and Nikki froze. "I have to go."

"Call me and tell me what you plan on doing about

this mess," Meg said before Nikki disconnected the call.

She tiptoed to her door and peeked through the peephole, to see it was her upstairs neighbor Winter, with her dog, Brooklyn, by her side. Although Nikki didn't know Winter well, they'd run into one another coming in and out of the building and in the gym on the top floor of the apartment complex.

Winter was a journalist, which immediately put Nikki on edge. Normally, they talked about streaming shows and books, and they both loved dogs. It was odd that she'd be here now considering they'd never visited one another before. With Nikki's sudden notoriety, she worried the other woman had a hidden agenda for showing up now.

Nikki kept the chain on and opened the door. "Hi," she said to her neighbor. Winter was dressed in workout clothes, tight leggings and a cropped top, probably coming from or heading to walking the pup. "Can I help you?"

Winter's eyes softened as she took in Nikki's obviously wary gaze.

"You saw the photos?" Nikki asked. Because why else would Winter be here?

The other woman nodded. "I thought maybe you wanted company?"

"Really?" Nikki asked, her sarcasm heavy.

"Honestly. Off the record. Nothing you say will go beyond us. I really just thought maybe you could use a friend."

Winter's warm tone and honest expression got to her. The kind gesture caused Nikki's eyes to fill with unexpected tears. With that one sentence, Winter was kinder than her friend Meg had been.

Nikki undid the chain and the dead bolt and stepped aside. "Come on in."

Winter walked inside and Nikki locked the doors again. "I'm sorry if I'm acting weird. I have trouble trusting people right now."

"I understand, believe me."

Nikki dropped down and petted the furry dog's head. "How are you, Brooklyn?"

The dog rolled over for a belly rub.

"We were going out for a walk when I decided to stop by," Winter said.

Nikki rose and she led them to the sofa. They sat down beside each other, and Brooklyn lay at her owner's feet.

"Listen, I get that things are hard right now, but it'll blow over. These things always do."

"Thank you. I hope so." She wasn't going to go into detail with Winter, the journalist, about the photos or her fear. Besides, there was no sense freaking out her neighbor about someone getting into her apartment.

"Is your family upset?" Winter asked.

Nikki narrowed her gaze. "Why are you asking?"

Winter stiffened. "I didn't mean anything by the question. *Most* parents would be worried about their children if someone tried to exploit them."

Nikki sighed and shook her head. Was it any wonder she didn't have any truly close, trusted friends? She was envious of Derek and his tight-knit group of guys. No ulterior motives to be found.

"You're right. I'm just wired."

"Can I make you a cup of tea?" Winter offered.

Nikki shook her head and glanced down at her shaking hands. "I had coffee. That was obviously a mistake. What story are you currently working on?" Nikki asked, eager to change the subject.

"I'm interviewing Sasha and Xander Kingston, Cassidy Forrester, and Harrison Kingston about their production company. As new as they are to the business, they're racking up awards and accolades."

Intrigued by the subject matter, Nikki leaned forward. "Really? I find the intricacies of what happens behind the scenes on a movie set fascinating. I wish I could learn more."

It seemed more exciting than walking down a runway and showing off designer clothes. Not that she was knocking the career she had so young in life or the other girls who loved it. Nikki was just interested in finding something different. In something more.

A knock sounded on her door, and she jumped, as did Brooklyn. The dog began to bark and Winter shushed her. Nikki walked to the door and glanced through the peephole again.

"Derek," she said, relieved. "It's my brother." She undid the locks again and Derek strode past her. "Did I hear a ... dog?" His eyes fell to Winter and Brooklyn.

"Derek, this is my neighbor, Winter. Winter, my brother, Derek Bettencourt."

He narrowed his gaze. "I thought I said not to let anyone in?"

"You said no one I didn't know. I know Winter."

Winter's smile was tight. "It's nice to meet you. I'm glad you're looking out for your sister. I'm going to take the dog for her walk. Take care, Nikki. I'll check on you soon."

Nikki nodded. "Thanks for stopping by."

Derek walked Winter out and locked up again before turning to Nikki.

She held up a hand. "Please don't start. She stopped by as a friend, and I could use one of those right now."

He nodded. "I know. I didn't expect to see anyone here. Are you packed?"

She nodded. "I just have to put a few things in my toiletry bag." Thanks to the travel involved in her career, she always had a cosmetic kit ready to go. "I take it Asher agreed to let me stay at his house?"

Derek put a hand on her back, and they walked to her bedroom. "It took some convincing but he's meeting us at the airport. He'll take you to the island and stay with you until it's time for you to come home."

"What?" Nikki spun around to face her brother. "You can't be serious. I don't know him, and I'll feel like I'm invading his space."

It was Derek's turn to hold up a hand, pushing off her objection. "I still don't believe anyone will figure out where you are, but I'll feel better knowing you won't be alone. I trust him. Asher knows his staff, and he'll be aware if anyone sneaks onto the property who isn't allowed. Do this for me?"

She frowned but couldn't say no. Not after her brother had gone to the trouble to arrange this getaway for her safety.

"Look at it this way. Mom and Dad won't know where you are either." His lips lifted in a smirk, and she couldn't help but laugh, too.

"Okay. I'll do it for you." She finished packing, and they took the private elevator downstairs to the garage, where Derek had parked his car.

At his direction, she lay down on back seat so when he pulled out of the parking garage, none of the paparazzi lurking with cameras could see her. He waited until he was certain they weren't followed before telling her she could sit up.

On the ride to the airport, she remained silent, her thoughts consumed with her host. She was well aware Asher had to be talked into staying with her on the island. Why would he want to babysit her because she'd ended up with naked photos splashed on the internet?

As they pulled into the airport hangar, she could add one more word to describe what she was feeling. *Nervous* to face Asher Dare.

Read **Just One Taste**.

Want even more Carly books?

CARLY'S BOOKLIST by Series – visit:
https://www.carlyphillips.com/CPBooklist

Sign up for Carly's Newsletter:
https://www.carlyphillips.com/CPNewsletter

Join Carly's Corner on Facebook:
https://www.carlyphillips.com/CarlysCorner

Carly on Facebook:
https://www.carlyphillips.com/CPFanpage

Carly on Instagram:
https://www.carlyphillips.com/CPInstagram

Carly's Booklist

The Dare Series

Dare to Love Series
Book 1: Dare to Love (Ian & Riley)
Book 2: Dare to Desire (Alex & Madison)
Book 3: Dare to Touch (Dylan & Olivia)
Book 4: Dare to Hold (Scott & Meg)
Book 5: Dare to Rock (Avery & Grey)
Book 6: Dare to Take (Tyler & Ella)
A Very Dare Christmas – Short Story (Ian & Riley)

* *Sienna Dare gets together with Ethan Knight in* **The Knight Brothers** *(Dare Me Tonight).*

* *Jason Dare gets together with Faith in the* **Sexy Series** *(More Than Sexy).*

Dare NY Series (NY Dare Cousins)
Book 1: Dare to Surrender (Gabe & Isabelle)
Book 2: Dare to Submit (Decklan & Amanda)
Book 3: Dare to Seduce (Max & Lucy)

The Knight Brothers
Book 1: Take Me Again (Sebastian & Ashley)
Book 2: Take Me Down (Parker & Emily)
Book 3: Dare Me Tonight (Ethan Knight & Sienna Dare)
Novella: Take The Bride (Sierra & Ryder)
Take Me Now – Short Story (Harper & Matt)

The Sexy Series
Book 1: More Than Sexy (Jason Dare & Faith)
Book 2: Twice As Sexy (Tanner & Scarlett)
Book 3: Better Than Sexy (Landon & Vivienne)
Novella: Sexy Love (Shane & Amber)

Dare Nation
Book 1: Dare to Resist (Austin & Quinn)
Book 2: Dare to Tempt (Damon & Evie)
Book 3: Dare to Play (Jaxon & Macy)
Book 4: Dare to Stay (Brandon & Willow)
Novella: Dare to Tease (Hudson & Brianne)

* Paul Dare's sperm donor kids

Kingston Family
Book 1: Just One Night (Linc Kingston & Jordan Greene)
Book 2: Just One Scandal (Chloe Kingston & Beck Daniels)
Book 3: Just One Chance (Xander Kingston & Sasha Keaton)
Book 4: Just One Spark (Dash Kingston & Cassidy Forrester)
Book 5: Just One Wish (Axel Forrester)
Book 6: Just One Dare (Aurora Kingston & Nick Dare)
Book 7: Just One Kiss
Book 8: Just One Taste

For the most recent Carly books, visit CARLY'S BOOKLIST page
www.carlyphillips.com/CPBooklist

Other Indie Series

Billionaire Bad Boys

Book 1: Going Down Easy

Book 2: Going Down Hard

Book 3: Going Down Fast

Book 4: Going In Deep

Going Down Again – Short Story

Hot Heroes Series

Book 1: Touch You Now

Book 2: Hold You Now

Book 3: Need You Now

Book 4: Want You Now

Bodyguard Bad Boys

Book 1: Rock Me

Book 2: Tempt Me

Novella: His To Protect

For the most recent Carly books, visit CARLY'S
BOOKLIST page

www.carlyphillips.com/CPBooklist

Carly's Originally Traditionally Published Books

Serendipity Series

Book 1: Serendipity

Book 2: Destiny

Book 3: Karma

Serendipity's Finest Series

Book 1: Perfect Fling

Book 2: Perfect Fit

Book 3: Perfect Together

Serendipity Novellas

Book 1: Fated

Book 2: Perfect Stranger

The Chandler Brothers

Book 1: The Bachelor

Book 2: The Playboy

Book 3: The Heartbreaker

Hot Zone

Book 1: Hot Stuff

Book 2: Hot Number

Book 3: Hot Item

Book 4: Hot Property

Costas Sisters

Book 1: Under the Boardwalk

Book 2: Summer of Love

Lucky Series
Book 1: Lucky Charm
Book 2: Lucky Break
Book 3: Lucky Streak

Bachelor Blogs
Book 1: Kiss Me if You Can
Book 2: Love Me If You Dare

Ty and Hunter
Book 1: Cross My Heart
Book 2: Sealed with a Kiss

Carly Classics (Unexpected Love)
Book 1: The Right Choice
Book 2: Perfect Partners
Book 3: Unexpected Chances
Book 4: Suddenly Love
Book 5: Worthy of Love

Carly Classics (The Simply Series)
Book 1: Simply Sinful
Book 2: Simply Scandalous
Book 3: Simply Sensual
Book 4: Body Heat
Book 5: Simply Sexy

For the most recent Carly books, visit CARLY'S
BOOKLIST page
www.carlyphillips.com/CPBooklist

Carly's Still Traditionally Published Books

Stand-Alone Books

Brazen

Secret Fantasy

Seduce Me

The Seduction

More Than Words Volume 7 – Compassion Can't Wait

Naughty Under the Mistletoe

Grey's Anatomy 101 Essay

For the most recent Carly books, visit CARLY'S BOOKLIST page

www.carlyphillips.com/CPBooklist

About the Author

NY Times, Wall Street Journal, and USA Today Bestseller, Carly Phillips is the queen of Alpha Heroes, at least according to The Harlequin Junkie Reviewer. Carly married her college sweetheart and lives in Purchase, NY along with her crazy dogs who are featured on her Facebook and Instagram pages. The author of over 75 romance novels, she has raised two incredible daughters and is now an empty nester. Carly's book, The Bachelor, was chosen by Kelly Ripa as her first romance club pick. Carly loves social media and interacting with her readers. Want to keep up with Carly? Sign up for her newsletter and receive TWO FREE books at www.carlyphillips.com.

Made in the USA
Coppell, TX
16 September 2022

83223115R00174